I0547363

Neo-History
Copyright © 2013 by August Hock
Copyright © 2014 by August Hock
All Rights Reserved
Published by MountainLion Press, LLC
www.mountainlionpress.com
2nd Print Edition –Corrected, Edited, Revised, and Punched Up

ISBN-13: 978-0-9890488-4-2

Neo-History

by August Hock

Prologue

A brunette walks along the dimly lit streets of Georgetown, arm-in-arm with a much older man. Their laughter echoes through the silence of the damp, empty streets. Water droplets linger on the leaves above them. When they stop in front of his row house, the girl steals a kiss before they disappear inside. In a moment's time, an artificial light shines through the window. Thirty minutes later, a woman's silhouette emerges from the house, closing the door quietly behind her, before disappearing on foot as a nearby church bell chimes midnight.

"Question the establishment, but also question the motives of its critics. Look beyond alleged neutrality. Everyone involved is self-interested on some level. Beware: Don't let another's selfishness lead you to your own moral ruin."

-Al Finkel

Chapter 1

What a horrible way to wake up. I'm all hung-over and alone. It was another night in a long series of nights spent without the love of my life, Angie. It must already be eighty degrees outside, and my apartment has no air conditioning. My sweaty clothes are sticking to my skin where I lie on my on bed on top of the covers. Scratching my scalp, there is a mess of greasy substance where there is typically shimmering hair. I know it's time to get up because I hardly ever set an alarm anymore. I feel around on my nightstand, but my glasses aren't there. Then I realize I hadn't taken out my contacts the night before. My eyes are excruciatingly dry, and I rub them to try to get some moisture back in to the lenses. In a single fluid motion, I sit up and roll off the bed to my feet. My lack of balance indicates that my hangover may be a worse problem than I had first calculated. Still, I make it across the floor of my studio to the sofa, where I drop on my ass and flip on the TV to watch the afternoon news.

The current story is about some legislative initiative that I've vaguely been following. Something or another about extending the protections of the 13th Amendment. I may only be 29 years old, but I've been around long enough to know this: Civil Right's gains and social disenfranchisement are all relative, conceptually speaking, both temporally and in severity. Once one group defines itself and wins the argument for need of special protection, there will be other groups being formed and marching along right behind their forerunner. Civil Rights movements are sexy and appealing to the conscience, which ensures that every generation will have one.

After the subject changes, a panel of social scientists are debating the disenfranchisement of organized religion. According to these intellects, religion is preventing them, the elect, from creating an unparalleled utopia on earth founded on statistics, mathematical averages, *reason*, and of course the scientific method. There is no more need for *spirituality*, or the code of conduct that has defined and maintained Western Civilization for 2000 years. "Nietzsche declared 'God is Dead,'" one of the scholars repeated two or three times, no doubt using the pre-modern philosopher's name to add *authority* to his argument. It's odd to me how quickly these geniuses have forgotten how contiguously the word of Nietzsche was spoken with the name of Hitler. But who am I to judge? The last time I took a philosophy course was in undergrad.

The news program finally postures itself to conclude its programming with a brief homage to a lauded scholar of history. Al Finkel died today at 79. I seem to vaguely recall his name from bookstore visits and college reading lists, but history was always too dry to interest me. After I finished my bachelor's degree in philosophy I went on to law school. From there, I worked for the FDIC for 3 years as a bank examiner. During my time at the Commission, I earned my Certified Fraud Examiners designation, or CFE. Because a CFE is virtually a private investigator of financial fraud, the District of Colombia required I also become licensed as a private eye. This well-equipped me, because after the Federal Budget Sequester and ensuing government cutbacks, under the old maxim "last man hired first man fired," I found myself involuntarily situated in the private labor market. As it turns out, it hasn't been as difficult of a transition as one might imagine. With my credentials, I have the potential to make more from one case than the Commission paid me for a year's work. Of course, that's only if I'm working steadily. The pluses are that I'm my own boss, I set my own schedule, and all that jazz. I even have a concealed weapons permit for Washington, and I cannot even stress to you how much regulatory hoop-jumping I had to go through to get that piece of paper. I don't have any sort of to-do list for the day, so I'll likely squander my afternoon scavenging for food and trying to keep myself entertained enough to ward off the depression. Such an itinerary, unfortunately, has become a relatively familiar daily routine for me.

Just as I consider making myself presentable enough to walk down the street and grab a burrito, the phone rings. I glance down at my phone screen to see an unfamiliar phone number.

"Hello, this is Wylie Wainwright," I say.

"Hello Mr. Wainwright. Please hold for Aaron Stevens and Lulu Chickabee," the speaker says.

"Sure." A moment elapses before I'm reconnected.

"Hello," a man's voice says, "you've got Aaron and Lulu here. We're the principals of Pioneer Publishing."

"Hi," I say.

"Hello darling," a woman's voice says.

"Hello to both of you. Without being too direct, how may I help you this afternoon?"

"Well old sport I'm afraid this is a business call. A rather sensitive, urgent matter. It's come to our attention that you have some expertise in gathering information in a discreet manner. Am I correct?" Aaron asks.

"Yes, I often like to say that I'm overqualified to handle these matters," I say. Being hungover can really make me quite arrogant.

"Then you would appreciate that this is the sort of matter that requires a face-to-face meeting?" Aaron asks.

"Certainly," I say.

"Our offices are on 17th and K. How quickly can you meet us here?"

"Well I'm in Glover Park now. I'd need a few minutes to gather my things. Let's say one hour?" I say.

"Make it forty-five minutes," Lulu says. "See you then darling." Then the line goes dead.

I'm suddenly cognizant of my putrid state again. Maybe I should blow off these needy bastards?

I've never actually done a *real* detective's case before. Well that's not exactly true. Once, when I was twelve, someone stole my bike. Or at least I *suspected* it was stolen. I marched around the neighborhood asking passersbyers if they had seen it. Finally, someone divulged that they had seen a kid riding a blue Huffy about four blocks away. I narrowed down the list of suspects immediately. I knew where a small list of bullies lived on that street four blocks away, kids I went to school with. Criminal types. The next day I snuck around their place, peeping in windows and such. I didn't turn up anything at their house, but on my way home I spotted my bike resting against a tree. Those twerps were about a hundred yards away throwing rocks at the windows of a condemnable building. I'd never done anything so brazen before, but I just hopped on my bike and started peddling. "Hey!" One of the kids yelled. But I was already sailing away. My parents saw me all excited and out of breath when I returned home; they made me tell them what happened. After I spilled the beans, they called those twerps parents to make sure their kids didn't retaliate for me taking back my bike. Those kids never said a word to me, probably having been informed they could have been sent to juvy for stealing my ride, but I did catch some crooked looks from them when I saw them around for months after the incident.

I flip open my calendar to see I've got absolutely nothing planned for the rest of the day and that this potential case, being as far out of my field of expertise as it may be, is likely to be the most excitement I'll have all day. I toss the calendar back across the coffee table, ease myself off the couch and in to the bathroom. A closer inspection in the mirror tells me this gangly creature needs a shave and a copious amount of exercise. Looking at me now, I think my entrepreneurial success might be the beginning of my demise. Once a guy has had a bath and some fresh air, it is actually a pretty nice day outside. I start down the street for my car, but the bus arrives just as I do. I quickly step on the 31 to downtown and swipe my smart pass. Two stops down the route I regret having not driven. Public transportation is going to make me late.

An hour and fifteen minutes after the phone conversation, I'm breezing in to the lobby of Pioneer Publishing. I sign in at the information desk and ride the elevator up to the ninth floor. When I get off the elevator at the ultra chic office, I'm greeted by the first voice I heard this morning.

"Mr. Wainwright, I presume?" this fine-looking brunette says.

"That's me," I reply.

"Hello, I'm Carla Allen, junior publicist. Would you follow me this way please? They're waiting on you," Carla says. Lord, as she turns and gives me a preview of her back side, I know how badly I'd rather spend the rest of the afternoon investigating Carla. First, I'd lead in with some introductory questions, some get-to-know-yous, and build a little trust. Second, I'd move in for some hard biographical information. During these first two phases I

7

calibrate her for nervousness. Then, in the third phase, I'll assess her integrity. If she's lied about anything, then I'll likely pick up on it. I'm a human lie detector. Although I don't suspect Carla of any criminal acts, if I did, I would seek an admission in the fourth phase. If the third and fourth phases are unnecessary, then I'll simply conclude my line of questioning and from there hopefully make an easy transition in to physical inspection. After I've concocted a crush on this girl, my mind can't help but associate the attractive girl with my Angie. Any wit I might have otherwise had at my disposal is extinguished; thoughts of Angie cause a decadence of the mind. It's difficult for me to view someone I'm physically attracted to as a spiritual creature when I've been so deprived of companionship during Angie's absence. I have been faithful because I do fully expect Angie to come back, but my sexual integrity has not come without a price.

"Mr. Wainwright," someone says.

I look up. Carla's hips must have hypnotized me. I wonder how long I was under. As a paid paranoiac, I can't help but wonder whether her affect was intentional. My suspicions are probable cause for an even closer inspection of the hypnotic device, but Carla turns it away and now she's facing me.

"Huh hum, Mr. Wainwright when you are ready," the man reiterates.

"Of course. You'll have to pardon me, being this high makes me feel a little queasy," I say.

"We're only on the ninth floor," the man says as he closes the door and gestures I have a seat on his sofa. An attractive, ferociously urbane lady sits atop a desk. Her blonde hair is cut short above her shoulders with bangs. Her black-rimmed glasses are connected to a thin pearl croakie. The amount of skin she is revealing causes me some embarrassment; in any even, I'm certain I'll struggle to not get caught staring during this appointment.

"Mr. Wainwright, I'm Aaron Stevens," Aaron says with a handshake before taking a seat on a chair directly across from me. Aaron takes a more traditional approach to style: gray sports jacket, red and silver diagonally striped tie, black slacks, brown leather belt and shoes. No flair really whatsoever, he's simply properly dressed to be operating a business. I'm glad I brought my blue blazer and pocket square along to throw over my white button-down and khaki pants. Aaron's hair is messy, but there are signs that it formerly, as recently as this morning, hosted some product. Most likely the stressful event, which he is about to reveal to me, only recently came to his attention; I would hesitate to speculate that what he is about to tell me has only happened this morning.

"Before we get started," Aaron says, "would you mind to tell us a little bit about your *credentials*?"

So he's pissed I checked out his junior publicist. Is his reaction warranted? Given the situation and the minor offense, I suppose it is.

"Certainly. I studied law at Georgetown. After I completed my time there I went to the FDIC. I was a bank examiner for three years. Last year, I opened my own private practice. I'm licensed as a PI in the District, but my focus is still on financial fraud," I say.

"Given your background, do you think your *up* to this job?" Aaron asks.

"Well sir, I haven't been given any details yet, but I'm going to go out on a limb and say yes. No matter what the case, it's all really about analyzing and following the trail of information," I reply.

"But what sort of experience do you have in this line of work?" Aaron asks.

"Oh ease up on him Aaron," Lulu says as she stands from the desk, and with a file in her hand, mesmerizes me with her approach and takes a seat next to me on the sofa, so close that our elbows are touching.

"Before we turn this information over to you, we *do* need your assurance that you'll keep it confidential," she says. Aaron nods in agreement.

"Of course. I still carry my law license. Everything we talk about in private is subject to the attorney-client privilege," I say.

"Well aren't you a valuable little thing?" Lulu says.

"I try to be useful," I reply, perhaps blushing.

"Here is the file. It should get you started," Lulu says. She opens it and places it on the coffee table in front of me.

"Yesterday our top author, Al Finkel, was found deceased in his apartment. We had advanced him a rather extravagant sum, or at least by our standards, for his new book," Aaron says.

"How much?" I ask as I rummage through some of the materials given to me in the file.

"Two-hundred fifty thousand dollars. Due to his consistent success over the years, we've permitted the drafting of looser and looser contracts. In this case, he told us nothing about the content of his latest book. No drafts, no requests for research assistance, not even a damned outline. We signed the agreement six-months ago and advanced the money to him at that time. The manuscript was due to be complete in two weeks, and when I last spoke to him he represented that the book was basically complete. He was found dead last night. I hurried over to his row house as soon as I heard. Because there were no indications of homicide or struggle, the police waived their ability to quarantine his home as a crime scene. I looked through every file on his computer. I reviewed every manuscript or book on his shelves. I didn't find a single trace of a manuscript."

"Now this situation places us in quite a quandary," Aaron says. "To have a total loss on the $250,000 would force us to report a net operating loss for the year. Now, even if he had just a rough manuscript, even if it is unintelligible garbage, we can still use Al's brand one last time to dump this train wreck of circumstance on to the unsuspecting public. *But we need something*."

"And you don't have the right to return of the advance if he doesn't deliver?" I ask.

"We may as well have not had a contract given how unprotected we are,"
Aaron replies.

"I see. So where do you recommend I begin?" I ask.

"Al's funeral is tomorrow. Alberto had many friends and influenced many more. His services will be held at the National Cathedral. I think you should attend and do some light snooping. Get yourself a feel for his universe. Today or tomorrow you should re-examine his row house with your professional eye. I hope you'll find a completed manuscript, if not, perhaps you will at least find a clue," Aaron says.

"One last matter. Although I sympathize with your cause, I'm afraid I can't afford to do this pro bono," I say.

"What is your usual rate?" Aaron asks.

"Five-hundred a day plus extraordinary expenses," I say. I'm always afraid my clients will lose their hat when I drop my rate bomb on them.

"How long does it usually take you to conclude a case?" Aaron asks.

"It really varies. If you want a thorough investigation, then I would budget for thirty days. But it may be more or less," I say.

"Thirty days? That's fifteen-thousand dollars!" Aaron proclaims.

"Aaron," Lulu says calmly, " I think it's in our interest to pay Mr. Wainwright fifteen to recover the perhaps million we'll make on the book, don't you think?"
Aaron's excitement seems to cool a marked degree. "Well Aaron?" Aaron stands, buttons his coat, and extends his palm towards me.

"Ok. Five hundred a day for thirty days. But I want a status report *at least* every day."

I stand and gladly shake Aaron's hand. I usually only get $300 a day. I don't know what came over me. "It's a deal. Of course, we'll be working very closely on this case."

Lulu stands and we shake hands as well. I can't quite decipher the little smirk worn across her face, but it's magnetizing. I collect the file, and Carla is promptly by my side to show me to the elevator.

Chapter 2

Sitting on the bus back to Glover Park, flipping through the pages of his file, I realize that the Professor had lived only several blocks from my apartment; a walkable distance. Taped right there on the inside cover of his file is a key to his house. I glance up to see we're crossing his street in this very moment, Reservoir. Quickly I pull on the yellow cord hanging above my head and an automated voice says: "Stop requested."

As the bus comes to a halt, I hurry from my seat and out on to the street. The Georgetown Public Library hovers immaculately above me. Looking back down Wisconsin one can see a giant swath of Georgetown, and even across the Potomac at the city-like towers of Rosslyn. When traffic finally ebbs, I cross Wisconsin Avenue and count down the address numbers until I locate Al's row house. 3636 Reservoir. It's as easy as twisting the key in the lock and suddenly I'm standing inside the dead man's home.

The otherwise dimly lit home is contrasted by the sharp rays of light that burst through the slight crevices between the drapes. After I open one set of drapes, I'm satisfied with the amount of illumination entering the room. Glancing around, I realize this is surely the pad of a lifelong scholar. The walls seem to be constructed out of bookshelves, and where there are a few patches of wall there hang artifacts and memorabilia of such wealth that the Smithsonian would be jealous. Two American Revolution muskets are crossed over top of the fireplace. Another wall hosts pictures of Al with perhaps a dozen various cabinet members from the last half-century. An umbrella stand holds a variety of antique swords, extravagantly carved and stone in-laid canes, a flagstaff that appears

13

to be crowned by a silver eagle, and of course a relatively plain but functional umbrella. There is no TV, but a basket next to the couch contains a rather rich collection of newspapers both from America and the World abroad. Leaving the living room, I find that the hallway is also constructed of bookshelves. There doesn't appear to be a single empty slot for a new volume anywhere.

The professor had a rather nice, spacious kitchen. Here, I don't see the first book. Perhaps Al was afraid of soiling the pages while he cooked himself dinner, dicing vegetables on his granite countertop and tossing them in one of his giant wok skillets hanging from a rack above his stove. Going back down the hall, I walk in to Al's office. Although books line the shelves and litter the floor, his desk is perfectly clean except for a Macintosh laptop, a one subject ruled notebook, and a cup full of ink pens. The one otherwise bare space on the wall displays three degrees: B.A. History, Georgetown University; Masters of History, Harvard University; PhD History, Cambridge University. The man certainly excelled in his educational attainment. I take a seat in his desk chair and observe a moment to take it all in. The signs of wear on both the chair and desk confirm that he did indeed spend a great amount of time here. None of the books appear to be for display only; they all appear worn and of historical character. I hope the notebook lying on his desk will provide me with some clue, but when I open it I only find blank pages. Next, I turn on his computer.

After the screen illuminates, I click on Al's user icon. Surprisingly, his computer isn't password protected. I give his desktop icons a cursory glance: course lectures, special lectures, academic papers, drafts, completed books, personal correspondence, travel and financial folders. I click the "drafts" folder, but the folder is empty. Next, I click the "completed books" folder, but the most

14

recently written book was completed well over two years ago—not the one I'm looking for.

Then I click on his email icon. It also is not password protected from this device. Slowly, I begin scrolling through the voluminous inbox, haphazardly reading emails hoping for a clue, and starring the messages I take the time to read. I read perhaps twenty lengthy, seemingly important emails before pushing my chair back from the desk and rubbing my eyes to alleviate the strain. I'm certain there's something in this inbox, but I don't know enough of the parameter of the puzzle for it to be useful at this juncture. I'm about to hang it up for the day, capriciously glimpsing at Al's bookshelves, about to hang the hope of the next clue on tomorrow, when I run across a framed picture of what must be Al and his daughter—or girlfriend? Al is weathered but sprightly in the picture; his large nose hooks over his lip, his dirty grey and brown hair has slightly receded from his forehead; his face is littered with enormous moles. He wears a thin pair of reading glasses. Al looks every bit the aged and wizened scholar.

Perhaps more intriguing than Al's predictable complexion is the girl beside him in the photograph. She's gorgeous, even for my standards: chestnut brown hair, electric blue eyes that shimmer in the flash, and arctic white teeth. She's an all-American girl, perhaps too young and alluring to be either Al's daughter *or* his girlfriend. I disassemble the picture frame, crease the photo in its center, and slip it in to my pocket for further review. Before leaving, I consider taking the computer along for further investigation, but given that I already have unlimited access to Al's home I determine it best to leave the valuables where they lie for the time being.

15

Chapter 3

The next day is Al Finkel's funeral. Today's stated objectives require what is perhaps the shortest commute of my career. Al's services are being held at the National Cathedral, which is just a few blocks up the street from my apartment. The ceremony is set to begin at eleven, and it's already eleven o'five when I cross Wisconsin Avenue. As I draw closer to the church, I begin to gather that this is no trifling affair. Throngs of attendees are still scurrying to get in to the service; chauffeured vehicles line the circle outside the cathedral's main entrance. Memorial flowers litter the entire area. Eventually, after waiting patiently in a solemn line, I enter the cathedral's main sanctuary. Once here, it's apparent that the service has not begun at all. Choir members are slowly trickling in to their box above the altar, mourners are hastily being seated by overworked ushers. I find my own seat towards the back, so I can people watch as the guests enter.

To spare the family and friends the publicity of describing the hallowed ceremony, I hope it will suffice to say that it was a fitting ceremony for an accomplished, gentle man. As the ceremony concludes, I hurry down a side aisle to speak with some of the attendees who were seated in the reserved aisles. Lucky for me, it seems a lot of people are eager to stand around and chat. While shaking hands and offering condolences, I manage to strike up a pretty good conversation with a former colleague of Al's.

"I was a distant relative. I'm ashamed to say I didn't see him the last few years. He was always kind and encouraging," I say and rub my eye's to sell my lie.

"Yes, um, sorry for your loss," the man says.

"How did you know him?" I ask.

"Oh, well we worked in the same field. We're both published authors and local history professors," the man says.

"I'm Wylie Wainwright," I say, extending my open palm towards the man.

"Edwin Lockington," Edwin says. "What is your occupation?"

"I'm an attorney," I say.

"Very good. Well Wylie, I can't claim to have known your, um relative *personally*, but I knew his professional work very well. Celebrated scholar. Really was. Troubling end for such a gifted man. Rumors of dementia," Edwin says.

"Had you heard any whispers about his forthcoming book?" I ask.

"No, no dear boy. Rumor was there was no book at all. He was a brand. Of course these unscrupulous publishers are going to leverage his stature for profits, insisting he write even through his final hours. Now, I haven't even heard that as a rumor in Al's specific case, however, I've seen it occur enough times to believe that it's at least true on some level," Professor Lockington says.

Lockington is convincing. If I were an amateur, I might conclude my investigation here. But training and experience, perhaps matched with inspiration from my generous and guaranteed pay for the next 30 days, is urging me to push forward until I have at least completed my due diligence.

"Do you know of anyone else I could speak with? Perhaps someone who is both familiar with his work *and* knew him personally?" I ask.

"Many knew him well in his professional capacity, but both? He was a complex man. The zeal that drove his career was the

17

search for better, and if need be, more complex theories about why the past happened the way it did. In his private life, he shunned the upper-crust. It was my understanding that he enjoyed spending his time with a more common sort," Lockington says.

"Let me think," he continues, "There is *one* person who comes to mind. A young lady, his assistant. She's PhD track, though I can't recall her name from the top of my head. Easy on the eyes though, or at least as I remember."

"Is she here today?"

"Likely. But good luck finding her in this mob."

There are throngs of mourners in attendance. I decide it's probably best if I seek this *young lady* out tomorrow or the next day, after all the excitement has died down.

Chapter 4

During the afternoon following the funeral, I was able to identify Al Finkel's research assistant by performing a quick Internet search. Regina Damasio of Georgetown University. Former varsity tennis player at UVA, all-ACC. While at UVA, she was a member of the chess club, historical society and founding member of PEPPD (Physical Education for Persons with Physical Disabilities). Perhaps I should have, but I don't hesitate to email her. A few hours later, I receive a response from Regina accepting my request to meet. She tells me she keeps her office hours from one to three, and that we can meet after she finishes with her students for the day.

With my evening free, I decide to meet up with my good friend Carter Ellis. Carter and I were roommates in the dorm our first year at Georgetown undergrad, and we've been close friends ever since. Although Carter studied Accounting, today he is a handsomely compensated, over glorified salesman for an arm of the financial lobby. Basically, policy analysts generate ideas, and then Carter peddles them to Congressmen, bureaucrats, and other influential and sympathetic members of the political community. Where I'm criticized for being either too factual or detail oriented, Carter is praised for his elocution. Really, I just love him because he's always been funny as shit.

I pull up to the bar at Breadsoda around seven, and find myself waiting several minutes for Carter's arrival. A smile spreads across my face when I see him enter the joint. Cold beers sitting in front of us, Carter and I begin talking.

"So you're asking me about my day? Ok, well it started with a call from the office *before 5am*. See, I've been working the rulemaking for this sensitive subsection to the Dodd-Frank Act. Well, around 8pm last night the sub-committee adjourned their meeting and all us interested bystanders went home. Low and behold the crafty lawmakers and their bureaucratic minions all reconvened informally at a dinner at some you'd-never-think-of-place in Adams Morgan. Apparently, over a glass of liquor and a fine meal they managed to work out in ten minutes what they'd been haggling over to a standoff all week. To make a long story short, they decided to remove all exemptions from hedge fund registration, or in laymen's terms the end of the modern dynamic power wielding hedge fund. It would represent a dramatic shift of power from the private financial sector to the SEC and the CFTC. Hedge funds would be required to disclose *everything*: every trading strategy, position, and algorithm. With all that information subject to disclosure, the playing field would be leveled and in many cases the actual operations capacity of these firms would be neutralized. But I've bored you enough with all this detail," Carter says.

"My mission, which began when I hit the streets at 5am this morning, was to kill this new draconian registration rule," Carter says. "Congressman Johnson, a member of the subcommittee, jogs Rock Creek Park every morning around 5am. So, being the stalker that I am, I jogged down to Rock Creek Park, running up and down the trail waiting for the Congressman to arrive. I startled the shit out of the babykisser when I found him. 'Jesus Carter, are you trying to give me a heart attack?' the Congressman said when I found him. 'No, no no,' I told him. 'From my point of view it's *you* who's trying to give *me* a heart attack," I told him.

"Woah, woah, so you woke up at 5am to stalk and threaten a sitting Congressman?" I ask.

"Come on Wylie. This guy's damaging my reputation on a whim. I had to do something," Carter says.

"Ok, ok, but then what?" I ask.

"Well, he caved a little. You see, there's five Congressmen on the subcommittee and they were set to unanimously approve the disclosure rule at one 'o clock. I had to change three minds by one p.m. to kill the measure. Johnson said he wouldn't lead the charge, but if I could get the other two votes plus do him a favor, then he'd go along with killing the rule," Carter says.

"What did you promise him?" I ask.

"Well, we'll get to that later. By the time I'd finished with Johnson, got home and showered, it was six-thirty a.m. Next on my radar: Congresswoman Genovese. I don't know if you know her, but she's a fine freshman Congresswoman straight from South Dakota. She hasn't even been in DC long enough to be corrupted. She ran as a Republican, but she's socially conservative and fiscally liberal. She's spoken out against certain practices of the financial industry, but isn't necessarily against the financial industry in-principal. There's reason in her and compassion, and I needed to tap in to her benevolence," Carter says.

"Now, the information I had on her, I'd only gotten it from a brief, and to my surprise when I walked in to her office this morning I found not some moley hunchback with a Jesus cross around her neck, but an absolute smoke show full of long legs and breasts, with a Jesus cross dangling from her neck. I was lucky enough to catch her before her peace of mind had been interrupted for the day," Carter says.

"We started with introductions. She told me about herself and her platform. I told her why I lobby for the financial industry: to make certain that the laws that govern money merchants curb their reaching for greedy excess, while simultaneously allowing room for financial innovation and other programmes that might alleviate the worst symptoms of poverty and economic inequality. By 8:15am I had the attention of Congresswoman Genovese. I noticed she wasn't wearing any rings, and I used every weapon in my arsenal to my advantage," Carter says.

"I invited her to breakfast, and with a quick glance at her watch she immediately accepted. We walked out of the building and down to a corner street vendor for breakfast burritos. Along the way, I told her my concerns for economic dislocation. I told her stories of my visits home to Sierra Leone. I talked about suffering. I talked about the difference between a broad sword and a scalpel. I told anecdotes of pious businessmen and the good they've done for humanity. When she said goodbye to me at her office door, she instructed an aide to give me a business card with her private cell number," Carter says.

"There you go. Get in that," I say.

"So I had one to go. Congressman Gregory often obliges my requests, but he requires an hour or so of priming before he does. Unfortunately, one of his aides informed me he was in a confidential armed services meeting until noon, and having lunch at the ultra-exclusive Kimberley Grill afterwards. Kimberley caters to Congressmen and other high-ranking government officials basically by denying entrance to the manipulative low-life's in my line of work," Carter says. "Having expendable time until the Armed services meeting ended, I went to the bank and pulled out $10,000 in c-notes. I knew this baby was going to be a photo finish, and that

22

I was going to need all the grease I could get. Next, I needed to find out who Gregory was having lunch with, and I needed to figure out how to get in to this famously impenetrable restaurant."

"In my line of work, there's some tricks you can only use once. Once you do it, word gets out, others try it, everyone finds out about it, so everyone knows what to look for, rendering the maneuver useless. Well I had one trick up my sleeve for getting into Kimberly. During my time on the Hill, I've learned who's the goody-two shoes and who the bad kids are. A few days back I'd heard a rumor about this one particular Congressman's daughter getting drilled by someone on his own staff. Seeing as the Congressman is a hot head, it was a reasonable inference that the staffer would be fired," Carter says.

"So what was the plan?" I ask.

"Naturally, I hunted the kid down, convinced him that the jig was up, compelled him to conspire with his fellow staffers to ensure the Congressman would go to Kimberly's for lunch, then sell me his Capital Hill ID badge for $5,000," Carter says. Carter reaches down in to his suit pocket and produces a Capital Hill ID badge bearing his picture.

"Of course, I'm no counterfeiter or forger, so I called that guy we used to use in college for fakes," Carter says.

"No shit?"

"No shit. He's still operating," Carter says.

"Luke hooked it up," I say.

"He met me in thirty minutes outside the Capital with his *doctor's kit*. He took a picture, sized it up, developed it, and laminated it on to the real ID in about seven minutes. The house call on the rush cost me $450. Armed with credentials, I marched across town," Carter says.

"Your suspense is killing me. You've got your ticket to get in, but how are you going to convince this Congressman to change his mind in one hour?" I ask.

"Well I told you that Congressman Gregory usually goes along with me, but he always requires some incentive. Sometimes its horse trading, other times its as simple as buttering him up. When I took an unexpected seat at his table at Kimberly's, it quickly became apparent that the only thing Gregory wanted in the future was to pass the Hedge Fund laws. Oh, I offered trading votes for pork projects and gave him a menu of other sweetners to choose from—but Gregory simply wasn't having it. This late in the game, with all other strategies exhausted, I was left with one tool in the game—intimidation. I knew I was burning an otherwise perfectly good bridge—but the situation required it be done. I told him since he couldn't cooperate, I would be forced during his next election to match every one of his campaign dollars with two dollars for his opponent from the financial lobby," Carter says.

"How did Gregory react?" I ask.

"His face turned Satan red. There would have been a scene, if we were anywhere else besides the Kimberly. The simple fact that I, a lobbyist, was sitting across the table from him was I believe enough to convince him of the seriousness of my threat. After I sat there silently while he muttered obscenities for a few moments, he finally cooled off and regained his composure. In the end, the little lamb even thanked me for *my* patience," Carter says.

"So you won?" I ask.

"The motion was defeated three-to-two. Those other two poor clowns didn't even have any idea what'd hit 'em," Carter says.

"I envy you Carter," I say, clinking his glass to my own.

24

"Thanks Wylie, but *you're* the man. Why not tell me what's up with you? Working? Patch things up with Angie?" Carter asks.

"I actually started this new case. Somewhat interesting. A well-known historian passed away several days ago, and his publishing company is paying me big money to hunt down his last manuscript, which they paid him for in advance. Whether or not the manuscript exists is a matter of conjecture," I say.

"Mmh, mmh and how much are they paying you?" Carter asks.

"Five hundred a day for a minimum of thirty days," I say.

"There you go Wylie," Carter says, slapping me on the back. "Get that money right son. I told you this practice of yours would pay off."

"I've always appreciated your encouragement," I say.

"So have you got any leads on this manuscript? Why can't the publisher just get their money back?"

"Answering your last question first, there are two reasons I think. One, their contract doesn't entitle them to a return of their money in this event. Two, if I found it I'm led to believe the manuscript is worth much, much more than the advance," I say.

"Yo comprehendo."

"Hu?"

"I understand," Carter says.

"I don't have any hot leads yet. I talked to one of his colleagues who claimed there were rumors the decedent had dementia and that no book was ever written at all. But the guy has a conflict because after all they're competitors in the same field," I say.

"Hmm."

"I've got an appointment with his RA tomorrow," I say.

"Guy or girl?"

"Girl, but I don't see why that matters. . ."

"Wylie," Carter says as he throws me a swift punch to the ribs. "You dog. I thought you were dodging talking about Angie."

In fact, I have been dodging talking about Angie, but it has nothing to do with my appointment tomorrow. Angie and I started dating during our second year of law school, almost five years ago. When I went to work examining banks, Angie accepted a junior associates position at a prestigious law firm. A year ago, I opened my own solo practitioner's firm in a hybrid capacity in a niche field. Needless to say, for the first six months I was busy either drumming up new business and tackling cases, or stewing in my own self-pity for the lack of demand of Wylie Wainwright in the world. After those first six months, work gradually picked up. In the meanwhile, Angie is working late nights on the cusp of her office's announcement of its newest partners. We both know she's a shoo-in, but she's never been one to leave anything on the table. I like to tell myself that our individual career strife has been the sole cause of friction in our relationship, but somewhere inside of me I know that's a flawed theory. We've both changed, and it hurts too much for me to think about it.

"Nah, Angie is fine. We're just kind of where we've been," I say. Perhaps detecting the sadness in my voice, Carter must have decided to drop the subject altogether. But when Carter opens his mouth again, I realize he hasn't decided to completely drop the subject after all.

"Wanna go on the hunt tonight? Find some skanks and fill 'em full of wine and lies?"

"Not really what I had in mind Carter," I say.

26

"I understand that. Probably best for me too. I am going to sleep fourteen hours tonight!"

"Maybe I will too," I say.

Chapter 5

The next day I'm up running around my apartment, wondering what I'm going to say and try to elicit from Al Finkel's research assistant, Regina Damasio. The situation will have to be approached gingerly, that's for sure. Her proximity to the decedent is a clear indication that she's no doubt privy to important facts, but I can't fully trust her until she's ruled out as a suspect as the manuscript thief. Still, I need an approach. What excuse should I use as a purpose for the meeting? I could recycle the lame distant relative bit that doesn't seem to hold water in this situation. Maybe I'm doing research to gather information for the biography of the biographer? Or, I'm doing research for his publishing company I *believe* for the biography of the biographer. Now that's not half bad. It makes sense, isn't suspect, and leaves me with a gaping exit from the semi-ruse.

I've decided to look moderately professional, so I'm wearing a grey and white plaid sports coat with a white button-down and black jeans. Digging to the bottom of my sock drawer for a pair of black socks, I find buried a picture of Angie and I. In the picture, we're dancing at our 3L Barrister's Ball. We're both dressed formally; I in a tux and Angie in a little black dress with white pearls. I'm spinning her in the picture, and we're both so happy that we're consumed by a giggling fit. This was the life with Angie I knew before everything turned so serious. So coffee stained with so little time with so much control of our lives ceded to others, the many near strangers who began jerking our energy and schedules around like we were pre-adjusted to ignoring our God-given autonomy all along.

Now I have my liberty back, at the cost of unguaranteed success. I don't believe Angie, on the other hand, has ever made a gamble in her life: in her instance, it is both a virtue and a limitation. But I wish I had not seen our picture there in the drawer or anywhere for that matter, because now my mind is unfocused to the task at hand and it's time for me to run out the door.

It's a cruelly hot day to make even just the short walk from Glover Park to Georgetown University; unlike my apartment, at least there is a slight breeze along the way, although it may be offset by the direct exposure to sunlight. I quickly slide my blazer off and only hope that my look isn't entirely wilted by the time I meet with the RA.

Relying on my encyclopedic knowledge of the campus, I soon arrive at Harbin Hall. Inside, Miss Damasio's office door stands open, but she's currently engaged in a discussion with a student. In the hallway, a girl sits alone in a chair clutching her book bag.

"In line to see Miss Damasio?" I ask. The girl nods her head affirmatively. I lean back against the wall, look up at the ceiling and close my eyes.

"You can sit next to me if you'd like," the girl says.

"Much obliged," I say to her as I take a seat. Not a minute passes before a girl exits Miss Damasio's office and the girl sitting next to me stands and disappears inside the open door. I feel a sense of pending anxiousness myself, a feeling I haven't had since at least law school. In school, I hated office hours. These visits are such a brown-nosers way to the top—though a way to the top they are. Even with all of my perspective, I still almost exclusively made time for only mandatory meetings with professors.

29

I notice myself anxiously fidgeting in the undersized arm chair. Has just my mere presence in this environment caused my maturation process to regress? My coming here has inadvertently released years of long-ago repressed anxiety. Why am I so nervous? What's the worst they could do, fail me? And why am I so nervous now? What's the worst this girl can do? Refuse to talk to me? I must be in the wrong business if I'm going to constantly be leaping these self-imposed hurdles.

Now the friendly girl exits the office, backpack double-strapped over her shoulders, beaming ear-to-ear with the knowledge that this week's brownie points are secure.

The next words that pop in to my mind are "oh my God" as I redirect all of my energy to prevent my jaw from dropping at the sight of this radiant brunette vision that has appeared before me and is standing in the doorframe. She's white Caucasian, but clearly no stranger to the sun. Her silky chestnut hair is cut at her shoulders and parted at one side across her forehead. Her thick black-rimmed glasses cage her wizened eyes. There is elegance to her conservative dress; she strikes me as someone who despite her natural beauty, is determined to make her way through the world on the merit of her mind. When I notice the light spark off of her eyes, I recognize her as the girl in the picture I took from Al Finkel's office.

"Mr. Wainwright?" she asks.

"Yes?"

"Please come in to my office."

I don't waste any time as I jump to obey her order.

"Please, close the door behind you."

"Certainly," I say as I close the door gently behind me before taking a seat in front of her desk. Stacks and stacks of books litter the room. An excruciatingly bright sun shines in from the window

30

behind her. I squint and resist shielding my eyes. Her silence suggests she would like for me to begin our conversation. I can't help but wonder if she realizes how distractingly sexy she is.

"Thank you for meeting with me today," I start lamely.

"It's nothing. Dr. Finkel was a mentor, colleague, and a friend. What is it I can do to help you today Mr. Wainwright?" Regina asks.

"I've actually been hired by Pioneer Press, Mr. Finkel's publishing company, to do some research on his life. They're exploring the possibility of doing a biography on the biographer. Sort of an ode to one of their greatest writers over the years," I say.

"Also a way to commercially exploit his name one last time," Regina says defensively, crossing her pretty, slender little arms.

"Do you harbor some hostility towards his publishing company?" I ask .

"Not specifically. You're prodding around a fresh wound," Regina says.

"I see. A gentleman would have began this meeting with his deepest sympathies for your loss," I say. Regina gulps, seemingly swallowing her emotion.

"Thank you for that. I've lost people close to me before, but I knew Dr. Finkel both personally and professionally. I can't say I've ever really lost someone like that. His significance to me, well, it's been a devastating loss," she says.

"I can certainly empathize with you," I say.

"Emotions aside, you've come here to talk about an altogether different matter. I think what you're exploring is a fitting tribute to a great man. I am more than willing to provide you with the information you need to get the project approved," she says.

31

I can't help but smile. This is going to be easier *and* an infinitely more enjoyable process than I had anticipated.

"So you're at the beginning of this project. Where do you begin?" Regina asks.

"That's a great question. I feel like his work is already so familiar and speaks for itself. Obviously including the story of the man, I would like to capture a deep perspective on the motivation behind his work. For instance, how did he select his subjects? How was he able to manage so many variations of style and arrive at such independent conclusions?" I ask.

"You sound as though you've recently read his Wikipedia page," Regina says.

I must be blushing. In fact, I had stolen those lines from skimming amazon.com reviews.

"I was recently assigned to this research position, which may or may not blossom in to an offer to write the thing. I read a couple of his books during college, but that was some time ago. I'm sure you, on the other hand, have an advanced knowledge of his methods and procedures," I say.

"I've been pursuing my PhD under his tutelage for the last three years. His work and reputation in the field are what encouraged me to choose Georgetown. I have access to all his books, unpublished papers, a Titanic series of email exchanges and reminiscences of personal conversations. I feel like if anyone could, I could help you portray him accurately. Maybe we could even include a section elaborating on the strategy he used to write his books. He had a fine method, and he never shied from sharing it with anyone who was eager to listen," she says.

This *is* going to be easier than I thought. She's an open book *and* she's already bought in to this project.

32

"And you could do that because you helped him write his last books?" I ask.

"Well, I helped him write his last book. It was my first big project at Georgetown. I helped him write *Global Trade and U.S. Foreign Policy* cover-to-cover. The process was a brilliant hands-on education for me," Regina says. She's really giving me some positive body language now, and I feel like our conversation is primed to take the next logical step in its progression.

"It must be really marvelous to have such access," I say. "What were you working on the last two years?"

"Surprisingly, given his lifetime of scholarly rigor, nothing," she says.

"Nothing at all? He wasn't even as much as exploring the topic for a new book?" I ask. She shifts her body now; she's a little less comfortable.

"No, I mean he was getting older. He took some time to enjoy the release of his last book, going on tour to do book signings, meeting with top policymakers about the implications of his work and so forth," Regina says.

"But he was publishing scholarly articles?" I ask.

"None."

"So to your knowledge a man who hadn't laid his pen down in over forty-five years was, for the first time in his professional career, working on nothing?" I ask.

"To the best of my knowledge," Regina says.

"One last, perhaps sensitive question. Over the last few months of his life, did you ever detect any symptoms of dementia, Alzheimer's, or other memory loss?" I ask.

"Nope. He was sharp as ever up until the day he died," Regina says.

"Well, that's all I've got for now. I appreciate your time. I hope you won't mind if I contact you in the future for more conversations like this?" I ask.

"Not in the least. Just consider me an asset at your disposal," Regina says. I feel my knees quiver. Is she intentionally speaking in sexual innuendo, or is it all in my head?

"Have a nice afternoon Miss Damasio," I say.

"Please call me Regina. And thank you for contacting me Wylie," Regina says. She stands and gives me one of the more pleasant handshakes I've had as of recent before I leave her office.

Back at my apartment, three bong hits deep, I'm lost in thought. I've now got four working case theories floating around in my head. One, Finkel had dementia and he was unable to perform his contract with the publishers. Two, Finkel was able to write but chose to become lazy in the waning years of his life. Three, Finkel and Damasio wrote the new manuscript together and she stole it on his death. Four, Finkel wrote the new manuscript in secret, perhaps to protect it from Regina or Regina from it, and someone else has taken it. On paper, Regina is a suspect, but after having talked to her I almost feel compelled to rule her out. But is her inordinate beauty distorting my thinking? Am I subconsciously rooting for her to be innocent from this macabre affair?

Chapter 6

The day after my meeting with Regina, I send her an email requesting the names of Al Finkel's closest colleagues. She immediately obliges me with a list of local history scholars and professors. The list includes: Dr. Anthony Silviano, Dean of Arts and Sciences and Chairman of the History Department at George Washington University; Dr. Leon Kasowski, Full Professor of History at American University; Dr. Brett Chandler, Professor of History at the University of District of Colombia; Dr. Kimball Cockallo of Howard University; Dr. Jonathon White of George Mason University, and Professor Edwin Lockington of George Mason University.

I figure I might as well start at the top of the list. I pop off a quick email to Dr. Silviano, basically using the same cover story I gave Regina. As soon as the email was sent, I get paranoid about Lockington's name being on the list and having told him a conflicting story. But surely these guys don't gossip daily. Even if they did, I doubt my brief dialogue with Lockington merited commitment to memory. Still, it's time for me to get my story straight and proceed more cautiously as I get in to the thick of this thing.

When I hop off the Circulator bus at Foggy Bottom, it's hard not to notice how much more urban George Washington University's campus is than Georgetown. I hardly ever make it down here, being the Georgetown-centric brat that I am. I try not to bump in to anyone as I walk passed the always crowded Foggy Bottom metro station. Hot dog vendors, curio stands peddling silk neckties among other novelties, a newspaper salesman pushes a homeless-produced paper, and itinerant florists all comb the streets

35

of this busy intersection. I do my best to hurry away from the masses and on to my meeting. I'm constantly checking my map app due to my lack of familiarity with this area. My technology guides me to a rather opulent building on the campus; I hope this isn't foreshadowing what I'm up against. I climb the stairs to the third floor and walk down the hall until I see a large sign reading: Office of the Dean of Arts and Sciences. Through clear glass, I see an anterior room that houses a secretarial pool. Without knocking, I push open the heavy door and make my way inside. There are three desks and a sitting area in the room, as well as another door that presumably leads in to Silviano's office. Of the three desks, only two are occupied. Both secretaries are on the phone. After a few instances of awkwardly gazing about, one of them points towards the sitting area and holds up one finger, before turning her head away from me. It's 12:55pm now and my meeting is scheduled for one.

Gradually, I tune in to the secretaries' conversations. One is discussing the Dean's schedule; the other seems to be busy soliciting donations. The one who acknowledged me is the one working on the Dean's schedule. The other places one call right after the next without providing me even an inkling of consideration. I watch the time tick by. One o'clock. One-ten. One-fifteen. At one-twenty, a man enters the room through the hallway who I presume to be Dean Silviano. I jump to my feet to introduce myself, and also to make certain he doesn't disappear in to his office with me left sitting here.

"Dean Silviano I presume?" I ask. The man gives me a quizzical look, but accepts my offer of a handshake nevertheless. "I'm Wylie Wainwright. I emailed you yesterday about setting up a meeting. You said you might have a few minutes for me around 1 pm."

The Dean stares at his secretaries with hostility, but both know better than to receive his menacing gaze: they turn their backs to him and continue right on with their phone conversations. True, one of them had set up the meeting for today, the one who had taken the afternoon off to take her dog to the vet. But it was Dean Silviano who agreed to and subsequently forgot the meeting.

"I've got a *few* minutes," Dean Silviano says, showing me the way in to his office. "Mr. . . ?"

"Wylie Wainwright," I say.

"Have a seat Wainwright," Dean Silviano says. The black hair that Silviano has remaining is slicked back; his aura emanates an interesting mixture of blue collar rough and high-academic refinement. It's almost as if I can actually see a dual-personality inhabiting a single man. His expensive, poorly tailored suit isn't enough to hide the coarse, callused knuckles or the inherent meanness in his eyes. Yet he seems to exude a form of diligent patience rare among men: If anything, it's his poise that startles me.

"Forgive me, but I have a tendency to be direct when I have little time. What brings you here?" Silviano asks.

"I'm doing research for a local publishing house on one of your late colleagues: Professor Al Finkel. Given your stature in the field and proximity to him as a colleague, I was hoping you could assist me in creating an accurate picture of the man," I say. I couldn't help but notice Silviano half cover his face with his hand as I am talking—a suspicious tell.

"What is the focus of your research?" Silviano asks, dropping his arm lamely to his desk.

37

"We're exploring the possibility of a biography. You know, the biography of the biographer type deal," I say. Silviano relaxes a marked degree, even reclining against the back of his chair and smiling.

"A biography of the biographer! History of the historian! Well, he certainly had built a brand recognition for his pen over the years," Silviano says.

"So you would be interested in helping me get the facts straight?" I ask. Silviano smirks.

"Oh, I don't know whether I'd be of much use to you really. I'm familiar with his work, yes, but I perhaps only met the man a handful of times. He wasn't really the sort to fraternize with his colleagues. Besides, I'm afraid that what I do know of him is rather dull, with the possible exception of that assistant he courted around," Silviano says.

"What about this assistant?" I ask.

"Through the grape vine, I've heard she's easy on the eyes. I've heard rumors she was in love with him, and maybe he even had feelings for her but wouldn't return her, um, *affections*. I'm sure this is a problem she had never encountered before, having laid eyes on her myself a time or two," Silviano says.

"Why do you think Professor Finkel would repel the advances of such a presumably desirable young woman, especially if he had feelings for her?" I ask.

"Because he wouldn't be unfaithful to his wife," Silviano says. At this juncture, I take out my note pad and begin scribbling some notes.

"I didn't realize he was married," I say without looking up from my notepad.

"Well, I'm no legal scholar, but they'd been separated for years. Not his decision. Poor old man was chained to his sense of morality," Silviano says.

"What about you?" I ask without thinking.

"What about me?"

"Are you bound to your sense of morality?" I ask. This time, I observe Silviano clutching his armrests with both wrists.

"What? Are you referring to the ethical code written in a fairy tale book over 2000 years ago? No, no I'm far too sophisticated for that," Silviano says.

"Do you believe in *any* conception of ethics?" I ask. A survey of his cluttered desk reveals at least one well-worn copy of Nietzsche's *A Will To Power*. "Or rather, what drives or informs your ethics?"

"Mill's utilitarianism, to reduce what is in actuality a much deeper and complex thought structure," Silviano says.

"The greatest good for the greatest number, and each according to his own ability," I say.

"Once again, greatly reduced, but something like that," Silviano says. "Fundamental notions of fairness. Exaltation of science at the expense of irrational superstition. With the dedicated work of many, we're on the cusp of entering a new age of enlightenment," Silviano says.

"Your philosophy is quite popular among liberals of the moment," I say.

"Do you hesitate to adopt it yourself?" Silviano asks.

"Sure. I hesitate before a lot of things. People love the certainty of numbers, but according to your own logic mathematics are cut from the same fabric as superstition—the human imagination. Beyond that, there is a notion that certain numbers in specific settings are superior to other numbers in similar settings, but doesn't it all collapse in to qualitative judgments of right and wrong, or better and worse?" I posit.

"An intriguing argument you make, but fallacious nevertheless," Silviano says.

"Why?"

"Because scientists rely on the scientific method. They use empirical evidence, unlike the average religious zealot who clings to their scripture," Silviano says.

"Do you think it's fair to stereotype every person of religious faith as a denier of science? Is it fair to credit all the advances of civilization to science? Isn't religion, if you trace it back to its roots, the bedrock of civilization?" I say all in one long breathe, but Silviano hasn't been listening. He's standing over his desk now, which tells me the meeting is over. I should punish myself for getting fired up and squandering an opportunity for a more in-depth interview.

"I'm sorry to cut our meeting off just as the conversation was becoming interesting, but I'm afraid I have an important meeting across campus at two. Please," Silviano says as he walks over to the bookshelf and removes a volume, "take this book of Finkel's. At the very least, it is an excellent volume for gaining insight in to his academic perspective." I look down and notice a gold ring on Silviano's right hand as we shake hands. The ring simply reads 'AHA.' Book in hand, and basically being politely told to leave, I exit Silviano's office.

On the bus ride home, I allow my mind to turn off. It was an intense verbal spar I had back there. I don't know what activated my degree of advocacy in support of religion, not being particularly active in organized religion myself. I suppose it was Silviano's strident belief in the dogmatic 'religion' of science. Any psychologist worth his salt might classify Silviano as 'hyper rational,' or possessing an irrational belief in the omniscience of reason. One reason is, after all, just as good as another. Reason is also a derivative of language, and although language exists in its abstract representations, because of both their synthetic natures, they fail to capture the totality of any object they represent.

Once I make it home, I determine to relax for the rest of the day to allow myself time to deconstruct my conversation with Silviano. First, I need to dispel the hostile emotions that formed during that bitter little argument we had. Maybe I could see things differently if I opened the blinds and let some sunlight in. Hell, maybe a bong rip wouldn't hurt.

An hour or so later I snap out of a sort of trance; I've been intensely focused on a documentary about warring ant species. I hurry over to my desk, remove a legal pad from one of the drawers and begin scribbling:

Knows more about Finkel than he leads on

Suspicious, intent to conceal something

Strident Atheist/pseudo-scientist

Finkel plus Damasio affair?

Finkel's wife

Motive?

AHA

Lying across the room on the coffee table is the Finkel book Silviano lent me. I make short work of retrieving it and bringing it back to my desk. *Global Trade and US Foreign Policy in the 21ˢᵗ Century* by Al Finkel. I flip to the last page to see that it is 896 pages long. Fine print. Then I read the blurbs on the back cover: "A fine treatise on foreign policy. I keep it by my bedside," says the sitting Secretary of State. "Written with the calculation of Machiavelli and the heart of the Dalai Lama. This volume has done more to promote World Peace than any other deed done by a single man," says a famous champion of Civil Rights. Flipping to the front, I see the introduction was written by Lady Margaret Thatcher. I give some thought to putting everything else aside and devouring the book in as many successive sittings as it takes. Then, however, I consider how valuable five days or even a week might be to the progress of the case and decide to leave the book as a possible lead of last resort. Or insignificant. But more likely just a drain of time resources.

I've got this growing list of people to talk to. I open my email and draft a message, then I blind carbon copy all the remaining professors on my list. Then I begin drafting an email to the estranged wife, but I'm not really certain how to talk to her about someone from whom she is estranged.

Dear Zelda Finkel,

I hope this email finds you doing well. I'm sorry for the loss of your late husband, Al Finkel. Although I was a social acquaintance of Al's, I am also his attorney. I understand there might have been some friction in your relationship, but there are some matters I should like to discuss with you concerning his estate. Please respond to this email with a time that it is convenient to meet. Again, my deepest sympathies for your loss.

My sincerest regards,
Wylie Wainwright

Now, I guess for the moment I sit back and wait. I can't find the remote, so I use the button on the box to turn the TV on. I've already sat down and become comfortable before I realize I'm watching a political arguing show. They're discussing this damned revision to the 13th Amendment again. It's a man and a woman, and they're virtually at each other's throats.

"If I'm a blue-collar company man, on salary, aren't I virtually a slave anyway? A wage slave? I probably have debt, and if I do I'm literally a peon. My employer knows I have to work, otherwise I've got no income to service my debt. If I default on a loan I lose everything. For 99% of American families, this is a hard fought battle *every* generation. *Every generation !* This new amendment could *end* that. What it all boils down to is redefining a simple legal definition to make the largest grant of property rights from the government back to the people in the history of the country," the male commentator says.

The female commentator wears a disgusted look on her face and is shaking her head 'no.' "This whole proposal is beyond ludicrous. I'll tell you what a word should be invented for, a new word should be invented to denote how ludicrous this proposal is!" She says.

"Enough conclusions. Why?" the man asks.

"Besides the fact that we need people to produce things in order to live? Work is inherently necessary, res ipsa loquitor counsel. Do you realize what would happen if every one just quit working and tried to live off of the government largesse? It would foretell the end of morality in the world. The wheels of capitalism would come unhinged and we would descend in to a dark age," she says.

"But we enslave the lower classes to do our work for us. Don't you think that's wrong? Shouldn't everyone be given the choice whether to work or to live off of a trust fund if they so choose?" the man asks.

"Why would anyone work if they were given the choice? I may not have to work, true, but I do have to work to maintain my lifestyle. If everyone raced to the government dole, then it would be socially acceptable to do so, and no one would work, *ever*," she says. "Money has a lot of negative associations, but think of all that can be done with money. It dictates how we make our choices. It's an abstraction we use to grease the wheels of a robust economy. If everyone quits working, eventually money will lose its incentive effect to drive people to do work they otherwise wouldn't do. Our economy of specialists will *break down*. People will have to resort to spending their time fending for themselves being yeomen farmers and hunters, instead of learning medicine, art, engineering, accounting, and basically everything that is useful that has given our society the wealth necessary to even be having this conversation. But just because we have the wealth which provides us with the leisure time necessary to engage in these types of discussions *does not mean* that we should actually follow through with these absurd notions!" she says.

"You simply aren't open to progress *conservative*," he says.

"Errrh. You know you really burn me up. Progress? You want progress? Ok, well how about instead of extending the benefits of the 13th Amendment, we *repeal* the 13th Amendment?" she asks.

"Why would we regress to a state of circumstances where full-blown slavery is allowed?" he asks.

"Why, for many of the same altruistic reasons that you cite! Think about it. Everyone today is free, but if we repealed the 13th amendment that would vest in each American citizen a new property right—the right to sell his or her self in to slavery. Think of what they could do with that money! A father may sell himself and use the money to send his son to college, to pull his son up out of *wage slavery*. The money could be used to pay for medical procedures to save another person's life. We all "sell" our time; current law simply forbids us from selling it all in one profitable transaction," the woman says.

"But slavery is per se wrong! Let's think about it. Let's say I sell myself. Aren't I selling my children in to slavery as well? Is it fair for anyone to make such a decision for anyone else?" he asks.

"Well, your children would only become slaves if they were born after your sale," she says.

"Won't I be forced to have children?" the man asks.

"Why?"

"Because I'm a slave! What if a master rapes a woman? Or what if he forces a woman to have sex with other men?" he asks.

"I suppose these are all things to think about before you sell yourself in to slavery," the woman says.

"What if it becomes a social norm among certain social classes to sell yourself in to slavery for the benefit of another?" the man asks.

"I don't really see why that question is relevant. Now social expectations are formed all the time. For instance, my hypothetical future is merely an academic abstraction of the absurdities that accompany a major, neigh monumental change to the existing limitations to property ownership. Your argument, on the other hand, is in support of a movement that has very real support and scarily enough, may actually come to fruition unless good people fuse together to defeat the effort." she says.

45

"One minute," the quiet moderator says.

"One last question," the girl says. "If your proposed expansion of the 13th Amendment passes, would you quit your job and live off of the government largesse?"

"No I wouldn't. I'm not in need of any of the proposition's proposed benefits. I love my job. I'm only campaigning for the rights of those who would benefit from the enactment of such a law."

"Imbecile," the woman says. A faction of the audience erupts in uproarious laughter.

"Excuse me?" the man asks.

The television show now only shows the face of the moderator. "Well that's our show tonight. We'll see you next time on *The Debate*."

The whole 13th Amendment expansion seems like such a bizarre movement to me. It seems like only a few years ago I was learning about Lincoln's triumph, and now its expansion is being heralded as an innovative solution to financial and social malaise. If it worked before it will work again. Only that noise isn't always true; it isn't always true at all. Conditions and circumstances change. Prescribe one dosage of medicine to a patient to save her life; prescribe a triple dose and perhaps she dies. Maybe it could be done without harming the health of the overall economy. I'm no doctor of economics. Give the people their liberty. But another show is coming on now and they seem poised to endlessly argue the same topic, so I rouse the energy to stand and turn the TV off.

I glance around what has become a dusty, at times grimy, certainly unkempt apartment. Books line my many shelves and are otherwise scattered everywhere. Old take out boxes are strewn across the floor. An overdue utility bill lies on my coffee table. The futility of paying one-hundred dollars a month for *utility*. I'd rather spend my money on something fun. I give beginning Finkel's book a thought, but I cringe at what I'm certain must be the driest pedantic prose of the century. But then I sit down and begin reading despite my self-admonition. Thatcher actually provides a compelling introduction, and I'm sixty pages in to the body of the text when my phone starts ringing. Carter Ellis.

"Five-fifteen. Happy hour?" Carter asks.

"Uh, I'm kinda in the middle of something dude," I say.

"What, digging through sock drawers looking for dead grandpa's journal? Come on man, we gotta get you back in the game," Carter says.

Now Carter doesn't really mean to insult my work, he likely sincerely believes that looking for a lost journal is what I'm doing. And as far as my reintroduction to *the game* goes, he doesn't understand the complex nature of the situation I'm in with Angie. We aren't broken up; we're just taking a break. I guess I was silent during the time I was explaining the foregoing.

"What are you really doing? You're either too high to leave the house or reading a book. Or maybe both. Either way, I *never* get off this early, so you're coming with me," Carter says.

"That's what she said."

"What? Ah clever funny man. See? You've got some humor about you after all. Now don't waste my time. Meet me at Breadsoda NOW," Carter says and hangs up the phone. I guess it's not that unreasonable of him to ask me to come downstairs to Breadsoda, given its proximity. But first I'm just going to finish this last bong hit.

When I first spot Carter sitting at the bar, I notice he's dressed unusually casual for Carter. He has already spotted me the

47

moment I make my entrance. I'm halfway along my approach when I recognize that he isn't alone. Carter's brought two girls along with him. I remember now, too late, that Carter speaks literally where the common person would just be using a figure of speech.

"Ladies, this is my great friend Wylie Wainwright. Wylie this is Penelope and Ally," Carter says by way of introduction.

"Nice to meet you Wylie," Ally says as she bites her lip and pierces my comfort zone with her sex eyes.

"It's nice to meet you both," I say.

"Carter's a lobbyist. Tell us what you do Wylie," Penelope asks.

"I'm an auditor," I say reflexively.

Carter grabs my shirt, pulls me backwards, and whispers in my ear, "tell them you're a detective. It's cooler."

I turn my head and whisper in his ear, "but it isn't true."

Carter drags me two feet further away from the girls and speaks a little louder this time: "Hello, you're investigating a theft. Sounds like detective work to me."

"I don't know whether there was a theft. The thing might have never existed," I say.

"That's not the point," Carter rebuts. "The point is when a girl hears auditor, she thinks tax collector. Chicks don't get with tax collectors, but detectives get with chicks."

"You don't understand my situation with Angie," I tell him, embarrassed to even be having this conversation.

"Can I talk to you outside?" Carter asks. Then he cranes his head up and addresses the girls. "Excuse us for just a moment ladies."

I follow Carter outside, leaving the nicely air conditioned bar for the evening heat that has gotten so muggy you could choke on it.

"What's wrong with you?" Carter yells. "Don't tell me you aren't at least a little attracted to those girls."

"I'll admit, they aren't bad for a Tuesday. But you really don't appreciate my predicament with Angie," I say.

"Don't I? I hate to be your reality check, but didn't she dump you over a month ago? When is the last time you even talked? How long can you live under the delusional impression that you're *ever* getting back together? I mean I hate it for you, I do, but she used you. She used you as a crutch during the lean years, and when her ship came in she dropped you. She's a partner at Sarten now. She's hot shit. You, on the other hand, are only doing really well," Carter says.

I think my eyes are growing misty. Carter slaps me across the face. Then he does it again. "I'll give you something to cry about," Carter says. He raises his hand against me again, but this time I restrain him before he can hit me.

"Quit that shit," I say while clutching Carter's wrist in mid-air.

"Look dude, I'm sorry she did you like that, but let it be a lesson to you about those types of girls," Carter says.

"Which kind is that?"

"The *Angie* kind of girls. The ones that bleed you dry then leave you for dead after they've sucked up everything you have to offer. Really, your relationship with Candice followed the same trajectory: rising action, several peaks, and then a final devastating crash. If you don't get back in the game now, then I'm afraid you're going to lose it. Won't you get after it with me? I've already got a set of ducks lined up in there, ready to be taken down," Carter says.

I feel a strange surge of courage flare up inside of me. I know that Carter is right. We've got to get after these girls like there's no tomorrow. Fuck Angie and celibacy.

"Let's get back inside," I say.

"Atta boy," Carter says, patting me on the back as he follows me inside. The girls are still standing at the bar, smiling at us as we approach them.

"Hi," I say.

"You aren't going to run away again, are you?" Ally asks.

"No. Not at all. In fact, when I said I'm an auditor earlier, well I'm actually a detective. I just get so used to telling people I'm an auditor because that's my cover," I say.

"I didn't think you looked like a tax man," Penelope says.

So we all talk and banter by the bar. After a couple of shots, we decide to play ping pong. Then pool. Then shuffleboard. Then more shots. Carter buys a pack of cigarettes and we all become chain smokers. I don't know whether it's Netflix or my bong that interests Penelope in coming up to my apartment, but visit she does. We start off innocently enough on the couch. Then I can feel the couch slightly shaking as she wiggles towards me. I ask her if she has ever passed smoke, but she apparently decides we'd skip the formalities of easing in to intimacy, and cut straight to the fun parts. In what seems like a single fluid motion, Penelope sways to and fro as she crawls across the couch cushions, leans in close to me, and begins placing her wet lips against my own.

I feel myself being relieved of a great anxiety with each kiss; I realize that before this moment I subconsciously feared I would never kiss another girl again. Soon we're playing tag around my small apartment only we're tagging with our lips, knocking things over around the apartment, laughing, celebrating life, and finally finding ourselves snuggled in the bed where we kiss until we lose consciousness.

The next morning is not kind to me. At first, I think the previous night was all just a dream. Then I feel the pounding in my head, and when I eventually regain a scintilla of consciousness I realize that the loud knocking sound is exogenous and emanating from my front door. Without thinking, I walk to the door and look through the peep hole to see who it is. To my surprise, it's some old lady sporting a pink pant suit and $300 bouffant hair. I might have ignored her, but she's knocking persistently and gives no indication that she'll go away without being shooed.

"May I help you?" I ask after cracking the door open. And the old bitch just pushes her way inside!

"This is quite some pad you've got here," the lady says sarcastically as she inspects the empty alcohol containers strewn about. She freezes when she spots the bong. "So *you're* the one they've hired to unwind Al's estate. A common druggie. This sort of thing is exactly why I *never* allow *anyone* to meddle in my affairs."

Now Penelope begins to rouse in bed as a result of all the commotion, tossing over the covers and revealing a bare breast.

"You call that a woman?" Mrs. Finkel asks.

"Excuse me? You did just bust in to my apartment unannounced and without an invitation," I say.

"Yes, but I've been around long enough to know that people put on a show when they're expecting me. No, I wanted to see you *in the raw*," Mrs. Finkel says. Penelope sits up in bed and pulls the covers to her chin.

"Wiley, who's this?" Penelope asks groggily.

"It's just a client. Go back to sleep," I say.

"What time is it?" Penelope asks.

51

" I don't know what time it is."

"It's ten minutes past ten, dear," Mrs. Finkel says.

"Shit, I'm so late for work," Penelope says as she jumps out of bed topless and scavenges around the apartment for her missing braw. As it turns out, it's an unfortunate moment to be hypnotized by boobies; well, it's an unfortunate moment for many reasons, but the reason I care about most is standing behind me at the door in sullen disbelief. No, as it turns out, she hasn't been out getting drilled by a senior partner. She's been at work trying to prevent a father of four from being deported and separated this morning at 9am from his children and wife of seventeen years. The worst part is Angie never said anything. She never says *anything* when she's fraught with anger. It's a commendable quality for a professional, but to me it means fearing the worst for extended periods of time. Last time she didn't speak to me for a whole month. My crime: I asked her to pay the dinner bill. I didn't think it was all that unreasonable. After all, she makes all kinds of money and she picked the ritzy place. I'm a sheep when it comes to Angie's expensive habits, but from the look on her face of murderous astonishment, whether I or Angie pays the bill is likely to never be a fight again. Angie has dropped by to give me a surprise inspection, perhaps she's even wearing a sexy negligee under her unusually thick jacket given the weather, but I'll never know. She's found me with two women. One of them is naked. The other appears well-off enough to take care of me through the lean years of starting a business. To anyone else, Angie is a champion of due process. But not for me. In this moment, Angie is prosecutor, judge and jury all rolled in to one. I'm in the midst of receiving no benefit of the doubt. Then she turns and leaves. I realize she's literally just walked out of my life, my girlfriend of five years, the girl who I intended to spend the rest of my life with.

Then a smooch on the cheek temporarily suspends my infinite sadness.

"I left you my number. Call me!" A fully-dressed Penelope says with a wink as she skips out the door.

"I don't know what kind of perverted love triangle or octagon you're involved in, but it had better not interfere with the probate of my husband's estate!" Mrs. Finkel says.

"Chill out. Sit down. I'm not your husband's estate administrator," I say.

"Then *what* are you?" Mrs. Finkel asks. I walk over, shut the wide open door, then take a seat on a chair across from Mrs. Finkel.

"I'm an author. A biographer. A soon-to-be biographer, but I'm at least a researcher at the moment," I mumble, but my hangover is seriously affecting both my thinking and elocution.

"Well which is it?"

"It all depends. I'm researching your husband now. I've got a deadline for gathering interesting material to get the project approved. A biography of the biographer, if you would," I say.

"Al would never consent to having a book written about his personal life. Who in the world would even suggest such an idea? He led the life of an ascetic academic. Why a common rock on the ground would be more interesting to read about than Al. At least a rock gets *outside*," Mrs. Finkel says.

How to play this one. "You're husband had built up quite a brand name for himself. I'm certain such a book would fetch a handsome purse for his estate," I say.

"Hm, let me think. Well I hadn't quite thought of that angle. Come to think of it, I do seem to remember Al talking about a biography or a memoir or sorts being written one day. I actually believe I have some old journals of his in the safety deposit box. I'm sure some old journals of his would be useful to you, wouldn't they?"

"I'm sure his old journals could be of great use to me," I say.

"Then it's settled. I'll make arrangements to meet with you again next week. But please look presentable this time," Mrs. Finkel says.

"I had no idea you were coming," I say.

"That's life dear. You *never* know who's coming. Ciao," Mrs. Finkel says. Then she shows herself out. What a mess. What a goddamed mess! I knock a lamp off an end table, but I didn't push it with enough force to break anything, not even the fragile lamp. Morbidly depressed, and with my mind racing fast enough to guarantee no more sleep, I take a bong rip of last night's bowl pack, crawl back in to bed, close my eye's and just pray to God I can get a little more sleep.

Chapter 7

The last episode must have really affected me because for the next two days the only reason I leave my apartment is to eat. Even then, I only either pick up groceries or grab take out. Between sobbing or starring out the window entranced by metaphysical musings, I do manage to begin reading the Finkel book lent to me by Professor Silviano. Surprisingly, it's really good. I wouldn't have imagined that a book on *Global Trade & US Foreign Policy* could be such an easy, informative, and unbiased read, but somehow Finkel manages to master all of these much sought after qualities of writing. In just two days, I cruise through 200 pages of his work. Along the way, I learn much, much more than the modest title suggests. In chapter 2, in a mere 40 pages, Finkel manages to provide a striking portrayal of the troubling relationship between Wall Street and Capital Hill. He cogently explains specific relationships between corporations, their intermediary lobbyists, and the politicians. Beyond politics, Finkel delves in to social science to explain the importance of interlocking economies for the pursuit of global peace and stability. He talks about wealth creation, the socialist movement, and the eradication of poverty. Poverty *is* relative, but it is also much more tangible than an abstract idea. And Finkel uses the most lucid examples to illuminate his conclusions all along the way. Even after I put it down, I find myself thinking more clearly. I know it sounds strange to say a highly academic book is helping me take my mind off of the other day and Angie, but whatever works, works.

Now I'm probably halfway through Al's book, on page four hundred and something when I get a phone call. My caller ID reads Lulu Chickabee—Pioneer Publishing.

"Hello?"

"Where are we darling?" Lulu asks.

"Researching Lulu. I've made some contacts and conducted some interviews. Right now I'm reading Mr. Finkel's last publication."

"You're reading a book? We're paying you to find a lost book, not read. Read on your own goddam time. Do you have any idea where the missing manuscript might be?" Lulu asks. I hadn't expected this hostility from Lulu. She was so collected and seemingly kind the other day. I know she must be projecting some other frustrations on to me, but still, taking shit reminds me of Angie. And thinking of Angie makes me sad.

"We don't even know if there ever was a manuscript," I say. " You gave me a case without any leads. Hell, I don't even know *what* I'm supposed to be looking for. You didn't tell me the title or the subject of the book. Nothing. That's what you gave me to start. Now I'm just barely a week in to this thing, so you need to be patient. I'm setting up more meetings over the next few days. Now please have a nice day Miss Chickabee and do check back soon," I say, before uncharacteristically hanging up.

I skim through my email to see that both Leon Kasowski and Kimball Cockallo have offered to meet with me on Monday and Tuesday, respectively. I received an automatically generated email from Brett Chandler telling me she is out of the country on an extended sojourn. Edwin Lockington asks what matter I would like to discuss with him, and asks whether or not we've met. I respond to Lockington's email confirming that we have indeed met before, and

56

that I would like to discuss the possibility of my writing a book about my relative, the recently departed Al Finkel.

I receive a response email from Lockington a few instants after I sent him my reply. He says: "How nice to hear from you again! Of course, a man of Professor Finkel's stature deserves a biography. However, I am afraid I am relatively busy at the moment and fear I have little information to offer about the man beyond what's already available through the public record. Best luck in your writing!"

My first rejection. Boo hoo hoo *Angie!* Boo hoo hoo. My eyes mist up. I consider where in my apartment is the best place to lie in the fetal position? Bed? Couch? Bathroom floor? I choose the couch, but something pokes me in the back, a remote or something, no it's my cell phone. Looking at the phone screen I think about all of the people I haven't spoken with during my hideout period. Four missed calls from Carter two days ago. I thought it was odd he hadn't called me. He always wants details when I take a girl home. I start to call him, but everything is such a mess and I haven't really the peace of mind to explain the whole thing to him.

I get off the couch and sit at my desk. I flip open my notes from the Silviano meeting.

Knows more about Finkel than he leads on

Suspicious, intent to conceal something

Strident Atheist/pseudo scientist

Finkel plus Damasio affair?

Finkel's wife?

Motive?

AHA?

What is AHA? Those were the three letters engraved on Silviano's golden ring. I open my laptop and perform a quick web search. It isn't surprising that numerous organizations use the acronym AHA: American Heart Association, American Humanist Association, Arabian Horse Association, American Homebrewers Association, and the American Historical Association. I click the hyperlink for the American Historical Association. After I'm redirected to their website, I arrive at a simple, one-page website. There is a picture of a historical relic, apparently a challis molded in the shape of a cross. There's also a mission statement: "The AHA is committed to preserving the record of the past for use tomorrow." And at the bottom of the page, just above the border, is a portal for secure log-in. Unamused, I close out the page.

I don't even realize it's Friday until I sit down to write out next week's schedule.

Monday—Kasowski

Tuesday- Catchello

Wednesday- Mrs. Finkel? Journals?

My scheduling efforts make me think of the weekend. The weekend reminds me of Angie. Impulsively, I text her. I sit there staring at my iPhone screen expecting an instant reply to my "Hi," but none is forthcoming. While staring at my phone I become increasingly cognizant of how much I lost when Angie and I had our falling out. She was my best friend; we did everything together. Besides Carter, she's the only person I spent a significant amount of time with. And spending time with Carter is like riding a rocket: In the beginning I blast off and start flying, but eventually I run out of fuel, crash and explode. I've never considered myself lonely before, but this must be what I am feeling right now. For a flash instant, I envision a lifetime filled with this breed of isolated misery. It's a notion that really startles me. I mean scared shitless. I feel a growing urge to vomit, so I start towards the bathroom. I've already

58

envisioned myself dropping to my knees, lifting the toilet seat and just yaking in to the flushable water, but after I flip the light switch I see Penelope's phone number still written on the mirror in lip stick. My whole life I've lacked the gumption to just pick up the phone and call a girl, but Penelope is a different case. After all, we have made out *and* had a sleepover. Certainly few other activities are going to help me move passed Angie than just getting out there and dating. I'm too timid to call, so I send Penelope a text: "Hey Penelope! It's Wylie. Are you free any this weekend?" I put the phone down on the sink, and it buzzes almost instantly.

"I'm actually meeting some friends out tonight, but we would love for you to join us," Penelope's text reads. The phone buzzes in my hand again. "Ally says bring Carter too!"

"Where are you all going?" I ask.

"The rooftop bar at Hotel Graham," she texts.

"I'm not familiar."

"It's in Georgetown, on Thomas Jefferson just off of M Street. Hope to see you guys there at 8!"

A rooftop bar doesn't sound so bad, and even if Carter is hard drinking he's still funny as hell. So I text him: "My man. Down to hang out with those girls from last night?"

"When?"

"Tonight. Hotel Graham at 8pm."

"Sweet. I'll come by your place at 7. I need to talk to you."

"About what?"

"Strategy."

"Ha. ok."

It's about 1:30 now. I feel like shit, and I haven't eaten. If I eat now, I probably won't exercise. I dig through my closet for my running shoes and lace up.

I thought it was hot inside my apartment, but the heat outside weighs on me like a ten-ton atom bomb. It doesn't help that I trip over one of those giant cat-sized Washington DC sewer rats about a dozen steps in to my run. I feel so gross that I almost abort the whole mission in lieu of a nice refreshingly cold and antibacterial shower, but I reason that I need a good rejuvenating jog in order to be able to pull off a decent performance this evening. Up Wisconsin Avenue, I take a left turn on to Cathedral. I pass this giggling, short fat dude in a uniform, and I notice that every car on the street has a ticket. At the end of the long line of victim cars I spot a special, one-day only no parking sign that is relatively obscured by summer foliage. That loathsome man ruins this city for everyone. Continuing my jog on down Cathedral, I imagine the stumpy-fat-bowling ball standing on a stage hoisting a trophy high in the air: DC's finest meter maid. A *remarkable* accomplishment if you ask me.

At the dip in the hill, I turn down a hidden stairway and in to Rock Creek National Park. It's a veritable forest in the middle of the city. For me, it's a sanctuary. An escape from the asphalt plague and all of it's symptoms: traffic, noise, lost time, stress, and confusion. Time stops in the forest. My troubles are left behind me. I'm home. I pass a few old wrinkled retirees and their ever-pissing dogs before I find the backside of a split-tail tanned beauty. Aw, now here's a nice pace fifteen-yards behind this wonderland.

Back at my apartment, drenched in sweat, I realize I've left my keys. It's an unusually long time, like half an hour, before someone comes along who can let me in. In spite of all my shower thoughts earlier, I grab Finkels' book instead, crack it open, and plop down on my couch. Time begins to fast forward as I race across the pages. Without interruption, I knock out the remainder of Finkel's book. I'm left feeling like I possess a policymakers knowledge of *Global Trade & U.S. Foreign Policy*. I find myself left with this newly discovered urge to explore and read about history. I run over to my desk and purchase books authored by the history academics I either will or want to interview. $118 later, I've got an entire summer's reading list and then some being shipped my way. After completing my order, I glance at the time—6:15pm. I set an alarm for 7 and lie down on the couch to take a nap. I close my eyes and fold my arms over my waist before drifting asleep. . .

I'm no longer in Washington, but standing on a dark pier very near the black ocean. I'm surrounded by friends, and we're drunk and laughing. My ribs are bursting in fact, deprived of air, lost in the abandon of the moment and ever present NOW. Taking turns around the circle, it's my turn now. Only what I have in store for the group isn't a joke. I enter a state of deep concentration. Then it happens. I begin to levitate above the ground. No, not merely jump in the air with impressive hang time, but I'm talking about defying gravity. Everyone is drunk enough, or so it seems, to suspend their knowledge of the laws of gravity and get a real kick out of my stunt. My initial intention was not to float but to fly, but apparently my inebriated state is preventing full-launch. I begin to vacillate, losing traction in my mental battle against gravity. I touch ground once, then twice. I start flapping my outstretched arms as if they are the wings of a bird; the action works and supports my suspension in mid-air, but it also has the unintended affect of making my friends' coo and cackle harder than ever. Their hysteria causes me to lose focus of whatever ineffable mind state it is that allows me to upend gravity, and my feet fall to the ground. I feel displeased, maybe even a little ill, like I always do when I have trouble taking off in to the sky.

Church bells ring in my ear. My eyelids heave open, and I reach over to disable my alarm. 7:15. Shit, I must have hit snooze once during my nap. I pull myself off the couch, strip down, and begin heating the shower while I shave. Then I shower and dry. 7:30. I pull on a white button down shirt, khaki shorts and Nike's and hurry out of my apartment. 7:41. Carter never showed early like he said, but no worry. Just outside my place is a Capital Bikeshare. They must have just reloaded the station because I have my pick of bikes. I unlock one and soon the wind is blowing on my face and tossing my hair as I glide down Wisconsin. I weave in-and-out of traffic, just like the courageous bicycle messengers whose once thriving industry fell prey to the Internet revolution's chopping block. Oh shit, some dickbag runs a light heading north on 37th and almost tags me with his BMW. My vigilant awareness rises and suddenly I'm not weaving in and out of traffic so boldly. I speed past a series of budget suit shops, the Georgetown Inn, Martin's, designer stores, throngs of shoppers, designer stores, and then I merge unhesitatingly left on to M Street. Traffic is bumper to bumper and impatient. Pedestrian's saunter along the streets, their arms filled with bags of overpriced goods. They're mostly happy. *Georgetown,* their moods seem to signal ecstatically. I lock up my bike by the entrance to the Waterfront and begin making my way on foot to the Hotel Graham on Thomas Jefferson Avenue. On arrival, a porter holds the door open for me.

"Hello sir. Welcome to the Hotel Graham," the porter says. He's been inside no doubt hiding from the heat in what I'm certain is an intolerably uncomfortable black suit and tie.

"Thanks."

"Will you be staying with us or having dinner?"

"I'm actually hoping to hit your upstairs bar for a drink."

"Be our guest. First elevator past reception," the porter says as he returns his attention to manning the front door. The lobby is well appointed but small, short ceilings lacking the generously sized common areas that are ubiquitous in fine hotels, but of course I'm in a major city where microspace is a big business. Waiting for the elevator, I spy a second bar on the ground floor. It's situated in a windowless room and despite expensive furnishings it's relatively unspectacular. A tight but exquisite mirrored elevator with a baby chandelier hoists me up to the roof. When the door opens, I'm standing on top of Georgetown, hovering above the Potomac, floating in the air with jets inbound to Reagan National. I'm suddenly gripped by the anxiety that amongst the three-fourths crowded bar I won't be able to recall what Penelope looks like from my alcohol scarred memory.

Fortunately, I see an arm waving at a table nearby that's attached to a pretty Penelope, and my anxiety abates.

"How's it going?"

"We're great thanks," Penelope says. Ally is just grinning. I can tell she's thinking *where the hell is the fun one*? I take a moment to survey my surroundings: It appears as though the whole city is on display from this vantage point. A slew of 757's approach Reagan in a single-file line flying just over the National Cathedral. Leisurers boat on the still Potomac. Minnions toil away to the East on K Street. Northern Virginia, with his modern skyscrapers appears more urban to the untrained eye than much of the District. But Northern Virginia is only a distraction, a trick to divert the outsiders' attention away from the nearby true seat of power.

"This is quite some place," I say. "How'd you find it?"

"We're girls," Ally says. "We keep our ears to the ground when it comes to fashion."

"Oh, of course."

"Be nice," Penelope whispers.

Luckily a waitress appears suddenly, and her presence immediately dissipates an awkwardness that might otherwise have lingered indefinitely. Using the waitress to assuage my gap in both comfort and conversation ability, I am unnecessarily curious about the features of the extensive drink menu. I'm surprised at myself for how long I'm able to keep this going. Finally, the elevator door opens and I see Carter emerge, so I release the waitress from recollecting from memory every last one of the craft beers on draft.

"I'll have a Bud Light, thanks," I say.

"Boo," Ally says. I nod my head around awkwardly; there's really nothing else for me to do but wait on my saving grace to take a few more steps to salvage my situation. Then Carter surprises me. I shouldn't have been surprised, but it's just his nature I suppose. As soon as he sits down, Carter goes in for the mouth kiss with Ally in the very first instant of the evening. I say I shouldn't be surprised because Carter has reminded me an infinite amount of times of his first maxim: Always be closing. At first I thought he meant closing in the terms of sales, but then he taught me that everything in life is a sale. Whether it's business in any of its myriad of forms, or dating, or platonic relationships and friend making—everything in life is sales, and Carter is a deft salesman. Carter whistles at the waitress, points to me and then holds up two fingers. The waitress nods with mystical comprehension. Satisfied, Carter relaxes in his seat, folding his arm around Ally's shoulders, and proceeds to commandeer the conversation.

"Hotel Graham," Carter says as though he's nostalgic for the place, though I'm relatively certain they only opened their doors a few short weeks ago.

"You've been here before?" Ally asks.

"Yeah, but only for business. You know I bring clients and suppliers here," Carter says.

"What sort of suppliers do you need in lobbying?"

"Politicians baby. They supply me the influence the clients pay for," Carter says. He leans over and scoops up a handful of nuts from a bowl on the table. He's munching as he talks: "Be a good middle man. Daddy always told me that from an early age. But then I figured out that everyone knows that, whether they follow it or not, which is their own problem. So early in my college days, this rich kid tells me his Papaw's advice late one night. 'He sez erryone gotta be selling something. Errybody on a commission. Now do you wanna be selling toaster ovens or financial assets?' Then I thought about how much money the guys make on Wall Street, and I started thinking there was something to what that fool was saying late that night. Sell stocks and bonds, *unless* you can find something *even more* valuable to sell. And I did find something even more valuable to sell: influence. Power is control, but control is an illusion. Even the President isn't in control. You see, there's varying degrees of influence. The President, he's gots lots of influence. I have some influence in inventory because that's my business, but most people ain't got no influence at all. The trick is to position yourself between the right people for the right spoken reasons, then if you're clever you'll have lots of influence."

I can't help but notice that Ally has developed sex eyes for Carter now. She's scooting that bottom around, wiggling it against the cloth of her chair's outdoor fabric, making it feel good and she's thinking about Carter. Carter Machiavelli Ellis.

"So who's your client now?" Penelope asks. I'm unusually glad to detect significantly less arousal in Penelope's demeanor then in her counterpart.

"Well I'm afraid *that* information is confidential, but I'll tell you what's going on around Capital Hill if you like."

"I'm really confused about all this talk about the 13th Amendment," Penelope says.

"Well it's about debt, unemployment and the new American way," Carter says.

"That doesn't really explain much."

"The Democrats are trying to garner support for legislation that would provide for the largest grant of individual liberty *since* the 13th Amendment. Only this bill extends to all socioeconomic classes," Carter says.

"Well how does it do that?"

"It wipes out some of the oldest vestiges of class privilege and responsibility. The rapid pace of technology has made full-participation in the work force both unnecessary and impractical. The only people who want to work *should* work, and everyone else should be taken care of by society's largesse. The bill phases out debt peonage, it eviscerates wage slavery. In the future, everyone will have minimum income *regardless* of employment status. It's called the AFA Bill, or the Affluence for All Act. Think about it. No more social strife. An era in which meritocracy will reign supreme. Art will flourish. The wealth of the greedy few will be devoured, but society will become so idyllic that even they won't care that their vaults have been looted because it will have been done for the common good," Carter says.

66

"So what's keeping them from implementing this?" I ask. Of course, I'm sure that the simple minds of the many have yet to make the connection that the AFA bill is nothing other than communism described in flowery prose.

"The Republicans. The fundamentalist Republicans want everyone to work even if there's nothing to do because that's a good old-fashioned puritan value for you," Carter says.

"What rational ground are the Republicans standing on?" I ask.

"Ha! As if their positions are ever justified! I mean we all know how backwards Republicans are. You know how I know it? *Because we all know it*, unless of course you're a Republican. But I'm going to humor you and try to formulate their position. Basically, the GOP is afraid that we're currently only in a temporary demand gap for labor. They're afraid that if we legalize leisure time that when work suddenly appears no one will be willing to do it. It's exemplary Uncertainty Principle, fear of the unknown, take care of the engine that brought you kinda guffaw. In my honest opinion, they're only being political and actively looking for reasons to disagree," Carter says.

Everyone sits quietly, presumably either in their own little world or trying to digest the points Carter has just articulated.

"It seems like thinly veiled communism to me," Penelope says.

"Me too," I utter reflexively.

"Ah, you regressive southern honkies. Can't you see that this sort of social movement *is* the future? That we *all* benefit from this? Imagine: all your credit card bills gone. Woosh. Don't like your job? Quit. Shazam. A few people in this country hold enough affluence in their coffers for us all, but they won't even share a speck of it with us. That's outrageous and immoral," Carter says.

"I agree," Ally says, her eyes enchanted. "It isn't fair for so few to have so much, while the rest of us are merely getting by." From the looks of Ally's Louis Vitton purse, matching Tiffany's diamond earrings and bracelet, and Christian Louboutin shoes, I seriously doubt Ally fully appreciates what the hell it is she thinks she's talking about. I'm tempted to call Ally out on her hypocrisy, but I don't want to cause a potentially evening-ending stir that might preclude me from getting with Penelope again tonight. Unfortunately, just as I'm hoping she'll get quiet, Ally hits her liberal ranting in stride. Luckily, the waitress is circulating by us every few minutes now, and I take every opportunity to refresh my drink. Somewhere between Ally's jumbled pro-abortion, anti-Dick Cheney, anti-Duck Dynasty rants, I lose count of my beers. It must be apparent that Ally is preaching to Carter's choir, as he's leaned forward and hanging on every word she says, nodding his head up and down and saying "yuhun, yuhun" every five to six seconds. Penelope begins to look bored to death: we're both just sitting here having our views marginalized. We literally must have spent an hour like this, before Penelope finally stands and with a double head nod indicates I should follow her to the bar. When I leave our table, I don't believe Ally has breathed in over an hour, and Carter still sits there in rapt attention. Even given his lust for liberal political philosophy, he's a tenacious son of a bitch to sit there and listen to this neophyte ramble on for so long.

"Thank God we got away from them," Penelope says as I slide in close to her and lean against the bar. "I just can't take listening to such doctrinal, doctrinal *shit*! I'm mean geez-us, learn some social grace! Am I really supposed to sit there and listen to her all night *just* to impress Carter? I mean she's sitting there talking about utopia while being the most shallow, self-absorbed, conceited bitch in the city," Penelope says.

I place my palm on Penelope's shoulder and my other index finger on her lips. "Shh. It's over. Don't let them get to you. Let's just find a way to enjoy ourselves," I say.

"I know you're right. If they want to get all deep and bond over divisive shit, then that's their business," Penelope says. I swear I think I observe her release the tension in her shoulders as they drop, and it evaporates like the fog rising off the mountains on an Appalachian morning. Something silly comes over me.

"Hi, I'm Wylie," I say. Penelope smirks and blushes and places her hand over her mouth to hide her surprise I'm sure she knows not why. When we shake hands I feel a transfer of giddy energy and it feels nice.

"Penelope," she says without exerting the least bit of effort to conceal her accent.

"Tell me Penelope, what do you like to do for fun?"

"Well um, I'm a graduate art student, so I like to paint. I like to create things. In the evenings, I like to dance, and I always like the company of an amicable young gentleman."

"What do you paint?"

"Whatever I'm interested in in the moment."

Uncharacteristically, I don't hesitate. I look her straight in the eyes and say: "What interests you *right now*?" She reciprocates my gaze, and we stand there like a passenger boarding a train headed to a place he's heard much of but never seen.

"Right now?"

"Now."

"I'm not so interested in painting. I only paint when I'm sober," she says, before adding, "but I'm *always* looking for inspiration."

"What about subjects?"

"Any subject will do as long as I'm inspired."

"Are you inspired tonight?" I ask. The sun has recently set in the West; however, twilight still illuminates the panorama surrounding us.

"It depends."

"On what?"

"Whether your next question is to ask if we can ditch our boring friends so we can find somewhere to dance."

My arm dangles around Penelope's neck as our taxi driver outwits M Street traffic in pursuit of delivering us to DuPont Circle quickly. Even at this late hour, he's listening to a talk radio show in a language I feel confident I've never before heard, but maybe it's just the accents of the subject matter. I really don't know. A cool breeze blows through the cracked windows, commingling with the air conditioning to make comfortable what has turned in to an otherwise intolerably hot night. The breeze must have gone unappreciated on that rooftop. Now the wind rhythmically runs its invisible fingers through Penelope's hair, both revealing and concealing her beautiful face behind the silky strands at its will. She's staring not just out but up in to the sky, probably hoping to catch a glimpse of a star.

After we exit the taxi on the circle, Penelope takes my hand and I assume she'll take me to one of the usual clubs I've been to so many times during college or with Angie when we were trying to spice up our relationship, but I'm confused as she leads me away from all that, down a residential street. I'm hesitant to question her:

she's leading with such conviction. Finally, we come to a pause in front of a large townhouse on P Street, and she leads me down towards the basement. She rasps on the door three times. Are we visiting her friends' place?

The door opens.

"Seven five zero zero nine two four," Penelope says. The doorman opens the door and allows us entry. After we're inside, he immediately closes and bolts the door. At the end of a short hallway is an elevator door. There is only one button: down. Penelope pushes the button and the door opens automatically. We step on to the elevator, the door closes, and we begin to descend.

"I feel like you're being quiet," Penelope says.

"I thought we were going to a dance club. I didn't realize you were going to go all Men in Black on me," I say.

"Haha. Relax. It's just a private underground club. It's in a refurbished Congressional bunker," Penelope says.

"That's pretty cool."

The elevator door opens to a sea of people dancing one floor below us. Laser lights pierce through a relatively dense fog. What I can discern is two DJs synching the beats of entirely different songs by manipulating the original cut by a myriad of different methods. Aside from the rambunctious dance floor, there appear to be a number of more mellow couched-out areas back near the bar.

"Drink?" I yell loud enough to be heard. This time it's me taking Penelope's hand, leading her down the stairs and then through the usual elbow-to-elbow nightclub in what is this otherwise surreal location.

"I'm going to say hi to a friend," Penelope says as she frees her hand from my own. "I'll meet you at the bar. Gin and tonic?" I nod in servile compliance.

It takes me quite some time to fight my way through to the bar. The whole time I'm scanning, looking for Penelope, but I don't catch so much as a glimpse of her. So I stand there at the bar with two drinks being molested by the abstract bustle. I loathe being groped, whether or not inadvertently, by strangers at the bar. Thirty-minutes turns in to an hour. I finish two beers and cash Penelope's gin and tonic. It's impossible to look for anyone in this place. Despite my strong desire to play kiss-tag with Penelope again, and maybe even take things further, I begin to develop an even stronger urge to fight my way out of this place, go home, and get some rest. Fuck you nameless elite club, I think to myself as the elevator doors close and I begin to ascend.

Chapter 8

Sundays are typically not a good day for me; however, this one isn't troublesome because of a simple ordinary hangover. Physically, I actually feel fine, but . . . *sigh*. None of my friends wake up this early on a Sunday, and by friends I mean Carter. I sent him a text an hour ago at 9am, but he didn't respond. I guess I'm not so bothered by Penelope ditching me last night as I am by the ghost of Angie. This morning I fully realize she's infected every square inch of my apartment with her memory, and they're all happy memories. They're all goddam happy memories. They're all happy memories made inaccessible by the barriers of time. Between work and Angie there just hadn't really been time for much else. She was my girlfriend, best friend, entourage, and close acquaintances all rolled in to one. When we were together I didn't need anyone else. Now I've squandered my last chance at reconciliation on a night with a girl I'm not likely to ever see again. My longing for Angie begins to transform in to general feelings of regret, so I summon what scintilla of will power I have left to think about anything other than Angie. I don't feel like jogging, but there is *my* case.

Sitting at my desk, I flip open the case folder. Tomorrow I'm meeting with Professor Leon Kasowski of American University. I open my laptop and begin with a simple Google search on Leon Kasowski. M.A. in Critical Theory at Brown University. PhD in History from NYU. His dissertation titled "Danger at the Extremes of Religious Freedom" seems like a regular rant by the academic industry in support of their paranoid bias against religion. I read the summary of the summary of the paper, which seems to be centered against a Supreme Court case.

The First Amendment protections of religious freedom are among the most well-known and established protections of liberty conferred to the individual citizen by the U.S. Constitution. Any grant of individual liberty taken too far; however, may place not only the actor but also his fellow citizens' safety in jeopardy. This paper will explore the case of a Muslim safety officer who sued the Government, her former employer, for dismissing her for her refusal to remove her hijab (which Islam requires her to wear) while on duty. Along the way we'll explore issues of religious diversity, racism, and the corrupt influence that organized religion wields over society.

Geez Kasowski is vitriolic. I don't know if reading this shit will put me in a better mood or not. I check my phone: still no reply from Carter. How does that guy manage to stay happy all the time? I guess it's something I'll just have to work up to, or at least it's nice to tell myself that. I know I'm nervous because I've never really been good at being single. But shit, two relationships account for the past twelve years of my dating life. There really hasn't been time for me to spread my wings. Maybe it's not that hard for a guy like me in a city the size of DC. After all, there's bound to be a ton of single girls anywhere I go.

I leave my desk, walk in to the bathroom, and take my shirt off to examine the goods in the mirror. Not too bad. Not too bad at all. I mean, I'm no body builder, but I do work out. And I could work out more now that there's heightened benefits. I'm a slim guy of 29 with a good education. Unfortunately, Carter is right about my work. Auditor sounds scary boring, but I'm afraid detective sounds almost unbelievable. Maybe *Investigator* walks the middle ground. *Independent Investigator*. That's it. I'll introduce myself as

Independent Investigator, and if they want the boring details I'll give 'em to 'em. Otherwise I'll just leave it at that. Play the mystery card. I pull my shirt back on and exit the bathroom.

I've got three people in my life: one is dead, one has deserted me and the third is MIA. I want to go out and make friends, but don't you have to have friends to make friends? I mean some confidenceless guy rolling solo down the street isn't exactly who you invite to your cookout. I guess I could have gone to church this morning; those people always seem friendly. The only reason I won't go to church is because I don't want to confront the larger problems I'm facing in life. I don't know whether my weak little heart can handle a sermon in existentialism. I mean it *can* be comforting to get lost out there in the metaphysical ether, but there's so much random chance involved: I never know whether I'll end up floating somewhere serene or being knocked around in some turbulently terrifying place. Maybe I ought to just keep my feet on the ground.

There is alcohol, but I earnestly doubt whether I want to be drunk this early in the day. Smoking weed will only make me think more, and I need to turn *it* off if at all possible. Again, there's the prospect of a jog. Or a museum or the movies. Maybe the fine art museum wouldn't be a bad way to spend the afternoon. I'll get ready.

I park my car at Georgetown University Law Center, just a few blocks away from the National Mall. Leaving my alma mater, I start down First Street. A few cooks smoke outside the employee entrance to the Omni Hotel. A man wearing tattered rags pushes a shopping cart towards the nearby homeless shelter. He's talking to himself. Another man in rags meanders along a few feet behind him. The second man admonishes the first man for talking to himself.

The first man scolds the second man for interrupting the conversation he's having with himself. I hurry on so not to become involved.

As the Capitol Building comes in to full-view it appears as though a large demonstration has formed on the Mall. Their cries are inaudible, each canceling out the words of the other. I do manage to squint to read a few signs saying something about expanding the protections of the 13th Amendment. Being apolitical as I am, I shove my hands deep in to my khaki shorts' pockets and plant my gaze on the ground as I turn my back to the Capital and continue towards the Art museum, which is now in sight. As I tug open the enormous copper doors, my face is struck by a nice cool winter breeze. The sudden change in temperature makes me cognizant of how much I sweated walking here from my car. Glancing around I see that most everyone else is similarly wilted, so I decide simply not to worry about it.

Architecturally speaking, the museum building is a work of art itself. In the early 1900's, Andrew Mellon purchased the land, commissioned the building, filled it with some of the finest art from around the world—and then transferred possession to the Congress as the custodians of the People. To this day, it is truly a fine gift from the former captain of industry.

The gallery is usually an amazing sanctuary, a hint of heaven, only today it's operating at full capacity with throngs of tourists bumbling through its halls, uncertain of where to go or whether there's anywhere to go at all. Some clearly revel amongst this host of form perfected, while others see pictures of people made with paint and wonder what all the fuss is about. My favorite painting is hidden amidst the many rooms along the upstairs corridor, it's Leonardo di Vinci's Ginevra de' Benci. Painted in the 1470's, not a single brush stroke is distinguishable for a total effect that makes the painting almost appear as though it's 3-D. Tourists rarely find this gem on their own, but it's a favorite of the tour guides. Today the room is almost too crowded for its elegance to even be appreciated. Still, gawking tourists hold their cameras up high above their heads snapping flashes, taking pictures of they know not what.

The central rotunda is one of the most exquisite examples of neoclassical architecture I've seen. With the cascading water fountain, colossal stone columns, light melding through the eye and mingling with the hushed voices of the reverent tourist creates an extraordinary impression on a visitor. I take a seat on a stone bench back against the large encapsulating walls born of the same material. Sitting in a spot that is visually stimulating to say the least, I almost feel guilty for my occupancy of this great room. But a quick survey tells me these benches are in sparse demand, so I rest assured that my presence is welcome. I shift my attention from my immediate focus from Angie and my case to meditate on a larger picture, to the next several years and decades and my destiny. Who I am to become begins today. I may have to be single, but I do not have to let the information bother me. Similarly, I don't have to solve every case; I just have to work hard, accept payment for my hard work, and always strive towards resolution. . .

An announcement on the intercom: "Attention all patrons. The museum will be closing in fifteen minutes. Please begin making your way towards the exits."

I check my watch. It's quarter to five. Have I really spent the entire afternoon here in somber reflection? I shake the inactivity out of my knees before I stand and, and I actually feel pretty good. I've passed the afternoon pleasantly, and I've got a full week's work ahead of me. By the time I walk to my car and make it home I should have just enough opportunity to review some notes, cook dinner, and turn in early for a good night's rest.

Chapter 9

I'm predictably nervous Monday morning before my meeting with Kasowski. It's 9am and my meeting isn't until afternoon. I really shouldn't have fired up my water bong 15 minutes after waking up this morning, but I did, and now I'm super stoned. I sit down and scribble some notes and try to convince myself that I'm doing work, necessary work, and that this work is worth all my focus. My notes lead me to a conclusion I should have considered before I set up this meeting: what good will it do me to interview Kasowski at all? It seems like Finkel lived like a hermit, not a flamboyant flapper's era writer. Still, I've got to do something to claim due diligence; I've got to struggle through this doubt and waning interest to make sure I haven't missed an angle to this case. I mean, maybe Kasowski stole the manuscript so he could publish it under his own name? There's a possible motive for any of these guys. Maybe there was some professional jealousy, so they off'd Finkel and the manuscript has subsequently been lost to wherever Finkel was hiding it. Then again, maybe Finkel really did have dementia and never even started the book. Either way, these meetings are a way for me to vouch I've been doing something for this case. So I scribble down some character questions before I dress and roll over to American University.

My first impression of the hall that hosts Kasowski's office is that it's cold and uninviting. The stone construct is made of brown, worn hue. It gives the impression of a medieval compound; narrow windowless halls, damp forlorn staircases and an eerie unoccupied silence consumes my senses as I peak on the fifth and top floor of the gloomy structure. I'm walking around a curved, dimly lit hallway. There is a noticeable absence of doors. Then there's a yellowish light beaming from an open door. As I continue my approach I can discern a placard: Professor Leon Kasowski. Since the door is wide open, I step inside. I'm instantly somewhat startled by the contrast of having found myself inside a chic ultramodern secretarial room. Decorated according to minimalist guidelines, both Apple and Restoration Hardware products are noticeably present. The room, although brought to life by electricity, is unoccupied. I glimpse around the room for any clue or indication of what to do next, but finding nothing I take a seat to await the time of appointment.

A grandfather clock chimes sullenly from the next room to announce half past the hour of eleven. It's only now that I hear footsteps in what appears to have been an otherwise abandoned building. The door cracks open before the clock sings its last chime, and a thick-bespectacled bald man of short stature peers in to the room at me. He holds the door open only as wide as his face.

"Maybe I help you?" he asks. I hop to my feet.

"Hello, Professor Kasowski? I'm Wylie Wainwright," I say. Now Kasowski fully opens the door and waves me inside. He quickly scurries back behind his desk and takes a seat. He indicates with a gesture of his hand that I should have a seat in one of the two plush chairs facing his desk. After I sit, I immediately realize that my chair sits me lower and his chair raises him higher. The shenanigans of those with Napolean complex. Unfortunately, Kasowski's office blends with more of the overall gloom of the building rather than pair with the modern decorum of his absent secretary's space. Dusty books which appear doubtfully read fill the many book shelves. An upside-down cross statute rests on Kasowski's desk. I guess I've gotten carried away surveying the

Professor's office because I'm startled when he interrupts our silence.

"How may I be of assistance to you Mr. . ?"

"Wainwright. Wylie Wainwright. I'm a biographer."

"I'm not familiar with your work."

"This will actually be my first foray in to biography."

"What have you done before this?"

"I was an attorney for several years."

"Lawyers think they can do anything," Kasowski snarls.

"Excuse me?"

"Huuummmm. Who is the subject of the biography?" Kasowski asks unenthusiastically, as if the conversation is so vastly boring as to have already made him drowsy.

"The late Al Finkel," I say. Immediately, I see Kaskowski's interest pique as if he has either just received a shot of adrenaline or some frightening news.

"A history of the historian!" he proclaims. "I suppose you've just given me some hope that I shan't be forgotten after all, after departing this cruel inhospitable world."

"You've got a dire outlook in life," I say.

"I am an devout pessimist Mr. Wainwright."

"That's odd. I don't usually hear people claim they're naturally pessimistic."

"I'm just owning up to what I am. We all live lives full of unsatisfied desires and then we die."

"If those are the angles you tend to emphasize. The crazy thing to me about life is that it continues, continues, continues until it mysteriously vanishes back in to the ether of unknowing. And as far as unsatisfied desires, isn't it the dichotomy, the existence of pain that makes pleasure possible? It seems like a perpetual state of equilibrium would resemble Nirvana. Does anyone truly anticipate annihilation?"

"You think too much for a man of employment, but too little for a man of letters. Existence is nothingness. All of this is a freak accident. We were never meant to suffer; it's this cursed human form that facilitates both perception and comprehension of suffering."

"You sound depressed."

"Don't lecture me on pseudo-science."

"Isn't that what you profess?" Now that hit a pressure point. I see the anger flail in the core of him.

"History is an art, Mr. Wainwright."

"What is art to you?"

"An *educated* interpretation of past events through symbolic representation. Or at least that definition approximates my views on history as art," he says.

"The procedure you describe seems very susceptible to . . . *miscalibration*. What precautions do you take to make certain your work is accurate and weighted proportionately?"

"Well we are all only human Mr. Wainwright and therefore there is no *perfect* work. We don't champion our work because it's perfect, but rather champion it precisely because of its imperfection. The process of writing history is one of constant refinement. *All work* is a process of refinement. The accumulated wealth of generations has been largely created through refinement, or gradual improvement of procedures, devices or ideas already in existence. Our ability to transfer intellectual and material wealth plays a large role in what makes us human."

"What if an innovation proves to be more detrimental than beneficial?"

"Innovation never stops. I believe some social scientists and the masses call it progress, but true social recalibrations can have more unforeseen detrimental effects than net positive benefits. That's why it is important that such decisions are made at the top, rather than by the caprice of the masses," he says.

"What do you consider the *top*?"

"Intellectual elites," he says unhesitatingly.

"But might such a faction force its own idiosyncratic whims on the rest of society?"

"No. It is theoretically possible, but no. The World's intellectuals carefully scrutinize every proposition before introducing it to the mass conscious. Every angle is evaluated for prejudice."

"But aren't there forms of information that intellectuals are not privy to? Don't people with different backgrounds and experiences tend to view the same situation with lenses of perception that are often at-odds?"

"Some consideration is given to the thought of the common mind, but it's more a concern for their reaction than their opinion."

"Isn't that sub-humanizing most of the world's population? To say their opinion only counts if a new idea might stir them to a violent reaction?"

"No. We are the representatives of the totality of human intelligence, the final authority on any idea's longetivity or ultimate demise."

"Do you think religion's influence on humanity has run its course?"

"Not exactly. For hundreds of years its influence was imperative to maintaining the social order. Now with the rise of modern science, it is time for religion's influence to wane, but not necessarily be entirely dispensed with, yet."

"Why undermine its influence?"

"Superstitious thinking. War. Dogmatic worldviews. I could perhaps write an encyclopedic-length volume on reasons why."

"But couldn't your own arguments be turned against you?"

"How?" Kasowski snaps.

"Many academics and intellectuals today base their worldviews on some variation of classical physics; however, classical physics only apply to the heavenly bodies, or *what the eye sees*. Quantum mechanics debunks many of the myths of classical physics on a subatomic scale. String theory is humanity's best attempt yet to arrive at a Unified Theory of the Universe and it would also permit the existence of as yet unexplained super phenomena written off by classical physics as make-believe. You see, philosophy has not kept pace with the developments in modern science. Many academics are actually awash in the dogma of outdated science. The Universe is much stranger than the eye or other naked human senses can perceive. We only know today some small fraction of what we will ultimately know. We shouldn't limit ourselves to a world-view informed by centuries-old science."

"Physics has a trivial significance on the philosophical underpinnings of a modern enlightened academic worldview to say the least. Ecology is the truly significant science of the day."

"Ecology and physics are both different layers of the same onion peel. Ecology has its own significance, in some ways separate from the study of physics yet both are strongly connected, at least by mere existence. You can't simply discard one science in order to enthrone the other. How much any given science should inform morality, ethics, or law is also highly debatable. But to ignore the benefits of physics surpasses naivety: it's reckless. Aside from providing the most comprehensive portrait of the Universe to-date, the practical applications of physics has led to some of the most unanticipated, ground-breaking inventions in the history of man including: digital computers, telecommunications, satellites, CAT scans, nuclear power, electrical power, laser, electron microscopes, magnetic resonance imaging, modern semi-conductors and more. God as a man on a cloud is a metaphor, Mr. Kasowski. He exists in everything; he manipulates the life of man subtly through the situations in which he finds himself and his subconscious. Although he is not limited to such, he is more discreet than overt. Why? I do not know, but it's simply my experience."

"It's charming to be in the company of an educated mystic. Now I'm beginning to discern some of that Southern draw. A Bible belt boy. I'll bet you always listened to your momma when she told you to say your prayers. Did it ever strike you as odd that you were talking to yourself? Perhaps by today you're aware that such behavior is indicative of mental illness?"

"What's wrong? You've run out of intellectual gusto, so you've decided to get nasty?"

"I believe this meeting is over Mr. Wainwright."

"Thank you for your time," I say as I stand and walk away from Kasowski, exiting the building through the gloomy halls of academia.

After I get home, I quickly jot down some notes from my meeting with Kasowski while they're fresh on my mind. Of particular note was Kasowski's hostility. I feel a certain amount of pity for the poor troubled man. On my coffee table is a recently delivered copy of Kasowski's book "The Religious Wars." It is a thin piece of 210 pages, or at least it's skinny when compared to Finkel's voluminous works.

My initial assumption was that the book was written about the 11-13th century Crusades, however, after having met Kasowski I'm not surprised to learn that Kasowski's ambition for the book was to pin every War of significance for the last 500 years on religion. In some instances, to the best of my understanding, some devout religious men were at the helm of a war machine. In most instances, however, the evidence connecting religion to the cause of war is scant to say the least. Like I said, it's a scant book, and it's written more for an audience of lay consumers than knowledgeable experts. The disproportionate amount of rhetorical argument to hard facts is troubling to say the least. I'm left in great confusion, wondering how Kasowski can transfer the blame for the crimes of government perpetrated with products of science on to the hands of religion. After all, it is a slew of the Pentagon's social scientists, not Baptist ministers, who make the first argument for war. Also, why is the President who conducts War not blamed for his responsibility?

I'm troubled on a deep level by Kasowski's absolute certainty in the face of a plethora of contradictory facts. Now I'm not particularly religious, but why target a compassionate association of old ladies and gentle souls to blame for the world's violence? I'm hung on, maybe even lost in, these thoughts when my iPhone vibrates. One new message from Carter.

"Sup." The message reads. Carter can be so elegant.

"Nm," I respond mindlessly. A single *sup* is apparently all it takes to interrupt my otherwise deep thought, because I've totally dropped Kasowski's dogmatism from my mind and began cleaning my pig-sty of an apartment. First, I unclutter the place by reshelving books and discarding takeout food packaging and other waste. I take my trash out in the hallway and drop it in the chute. My phone buzzes again.

"Softball game at 8?" Carter's text reads.

"It's a little late on a Monday night for a softball game, isn't it?"

"Let's play. You desperately need to get out of the house plus the league is co-ed. There's supposed to be some talent on the other team. You gotta drop the high and mighty. You desperately need some socializing. You aren't cool enough to always be hanging out by yourself."

You know, I hadn't really felt *desperate* until Carter used the word. Now that he's used it, it describes my situation. Carter's word usage channels my mind to thoughts of Angie: our six-year relationship is over. Penelope Irish goodbyed me. I'm a soulless auditor for crissakes. When I reflect that all I have to show for my 29 years of living are my friendship with a degenerate like Carter and a handful of well-spun lies, I feel a dark cloud eclipse whatever emotional sunshine there might be inside of me.

Now I have a decision to make. If I don't go out with Carter, then I'm probably going to stay here and continue to *clean* my apartment. Subjectively speaking, my apartment is clean enough; however, if I decide to stay in I could always summon a neurosis to compel me to clean more. I could dust and clean the windows. I could armor-all my trash cans. Hell, I could go bat shit crazy and operate a vacuum cleaner for a few minutes.

"8 o'clock? That's like right now."

"I'm at the ball park putting on my cleats now."

"Let me clean up and I'll be right down."

Brush my teeth. Hit of deodorant. Fresh t-shirt, gym shorts, sneakers in lieu of cleats, and a Nats baseball cap. The ball field is a short walk away, in the park adjacent to the Whole Foods. On arrival, there's numerous people standing around stretching, swinging bats in the air, tossing baseball, and gossiping. When he spots me, Carter trots over to me with a team t-shirt.

"Glad you came out Wiley. Put this on. Welcome to the team," he says, and slaps me on the arm. I feel self-conscious to switch t-shirts in front of everyone, I do see a fair amount of good looking girls around, but I rationalize that I'm really in pretty decent shape despite my lack of muscle mass. I quickly take off my shirt and pull the other shirt over my head. The new shirt is too tight, but not so tight that I can make an issue of it. I guess I'm just stuck with this slim fit t-shirt for the remainder of the evening. "You need to head over and give your name to the score keeper," Carter says.

I walk over to join a small line of people divulging their names to the scorekeeper. The guy who is doing it looks real athletic; I wonder why he isn't playing ball.

"Sup boss," he says when my turn accrues.

"Hey man. Wylie Wainwright."

"Thanks Wylie. Which team you playing for?"

"I'm with Carter Ellis, I'm not actually sure what they call themselves."

"Let's see here, Carter is on the Liberty City Growlers."

"Interesting name."

"It actually came in dead last when we voted for best team name."

"What was the best team name?"

"I actually don't remember. None of them are really that witty."

"I see."

"Ok, you're on the roster. Go warm up and we'll get started in about fifteen minutes."

"Thanks man."

I start to trot over towards Carter, but he steps up to the plate to swing at a couple of practice balls. I don't recognize anyone else in my near vicinity, so I pony up to the bench, tossing a baseball in to my glove.

"Ok, let's get going," the scorekeeper yells. Some guys come trotting out of left field when I recognize several of them work at Angie's firm, Sarten PLLC. One of them is a particularly snobbish fellow, Doug Creekmore. I hope he jogs on by our dugout without recognizing me, but with my luck lately, I'm not surprised when he immediately recognizes me.

"Wylie? Right?" Doug asks as he stops just in front of me. He's the type of guy that wears his ultra-expensive tortoise shell eyeglasses even when he's playing sports. He's got that wavy red hair and thick freckles dotted across his face. He's kind of buff in his tight-fitting baseball jersey and pants ensemble, a quality I'd never noticed of him. He's the type of guy you rarely see out without a suit on.

"Hey Doug," I say.

"How are things over at the FDIC?"

"Um, I'm not there anymore. I set up my own shop."

"Hung a shingle ay? What niche are you practicing in?"

"Actually, I've transitioned into fraud examination and private detective work."

"*Private detective work!*" He says while he bellows in laughter, and places his hand on my shoulder, like he needs me to support him or he'll otherwise fall to the ground. "What a sense of humor!" He says after he collects himself.

"I'm really a detective."

"Ha-ha quit it. You got fired from the FDIC and you can't come up with a better excuse for yourself than that?"

Carter just happened to be approaching us and overheard Doug's last comment.

"You got a problem?" Carter asks.

"Why don't you mind your business boy?" Doug says in that thick Alabama accent with a dash of Yale pretentiousness. Carter starts at Doug, so that I have to hold Carter back. Being called anything *approaching* a racial epitaph enrages Carter beyond his senses.

"That's not nice," Carter says. "Didn't your momma teach you not to be so condescending?"

"What are you boys so riled up for? I mean, I know Wylie's probably still not over Regina leaving him. Don't worry Wylie, we're taking *good care* of her," Doug says with a pelvic thrust.

Carter leans back before his fist surges over my shoulder and in to Doug Creekmore's cheekbone. Doug falls flat on his back. The act causes a swift, chain reaction as seemingly everyone with a baseball glove lunges toward us, pushing, cussing, throwing punches, kicks, spit flies everywhere, a few do-gooders try to break the thing up but the delicate civility which exists between rival teams has exploded in to one great conflagration. After several minutes of brawling, the participants lose steam and the arrival of a two police cars officially ceases the remaining fighting. I take a few steps back after I've escaped the battle to see several bodies lying on the ground. In the distance, I see bodies fleeing the scene including that ginger-headed Doug Creekmore. He *would* run like a scared chicken. There is a rather large, bad-tempered cop up in my face now making me wish I had fled the scene as well. He's peppering

90

me with questions and I'm reluctant to provide answers about the events that transpired.

"I don't know. We were about to starting playing ball when there was a misunderstanding and someone must have started throwing punches and the whole thing just sparked up." The cop is somewhat pacified as he jots my words down in to his little notebook. "Hard to know who started it though," I say. "I'm just glad you boys showed up when you did."

He releases me to interview the next person. I grab Carter and we skedaddle on out of there. I believe we both breathe a little easier once we've made it out of the park and pass the Whole Foods, blending in with the rest of the pedestrians. When we hear sirens in the distance, we increase our clip to just below a conspicuous full-on run until we're safely out of sight in my apartment building elevator.

"Sorry about that . Just a little disoriented," Carter says.

"You're sorry about that ? What about the rest of the goddam spectacle? Do you even realize that I have to walk past there every day? We're lucky those Sarten punks didn't rough us up worse than they did."

"Sorry. Ok? Geez. A guy has one little lapse in judgment and you treat him like this? I bet you gave your friends a real guilt-ridden childhood."

"A *little* lapse in judgment? You just punched Doug Creekmore! Those pricks know who we are. In *my* neighborhood!"

"Relax. Listen. Just make yourself scarce around there for a couple of weeks and they'll forget about the whole thing. They have stuff like that happen in those places all the time."

"Carter, I've been playing baseball since I was nine, and I have *never* seen someone pull a stunt like the one you just pulled."

"Yeah, but you grew up white. Probably even playing in leagues. I grew up playing in the hood, where you either fought or got made somebody's bitch. I ain't letting nobody think either me or my boy is a pushover."

I unlock the door to my apartment and collapse on the couch. Carter makes his way to the bathroom, presumably to tend to his wounds. I still haven't fully come down from the adrenaline rush; my mind is racing across ideas, skipping from the brilliance of one mental illumination to the next. Then an image of Angie's smiling face blots out all other thoughts. All I can think about is Angie. Angie. Now she only exists in my imagination and the thought brings tears to my eyes. I know the real Angie is somewhere else, perhaps being entertained by another man or even plotting with a close friend how she'll mold a new life for herself without any room in it for me. She'll meet another man, and I'll be jealous. My jealous flare is a sullen reminder of all my failures. Failed. Failed. Failed. The thought of the doomed outcomes of so many of my best efforts makes me wish I had taken more time to celebrate and savor the successes. But the Zen inside reassures me that I don't labor for mere outcomes, but act as an end in and of itself. Every breath is a celebration of life.

"What's up with you?"

"I'm just working through some things."

"You're crying about Angie. *Aiggh!*" He yells out. "I had the best-damned intentions dude. I wanted to show you a good time, move you along through the break-up depression process, but you're regressing. I'm sorry Wylie. I guess I've just been getting my way so much lately that I just don't know when to stop. I don't have limits anymore, but it's that lack of knowledge that my whole personality, hell my whole career is premised on."

"Look, don't be so hard on yourself," I say. "We all have our off nights. Even lame prudish attorneys like me do dumb stuff from time to time. Even saints make mistakes man."

Carter's shaking his head 'no.' "Not me man. Flawless is my game. Perfection is merely the absence of mistakes, and *I fucked up man*," Carter says as his voice disintegrates in to a trembling whimper. "What if the wrong person finds out what I did tonight? They'll kick me out of the game! I'll love my job. I'll have to start a *new career*. I can't sell insurance Wiley. I mean I'm corrupt enough, but I'm too proud."

"Carter relax. You aren't the first guy to punch a guy before a city league softball game. Look, first of all the police didn't even get your name. The whole thing happened so quick that no one probably even knows what happened besides Doug Creekmore. And *everyone* knows Doug Creekmore is a dickhead. Sure, maybe you should steer clear of his zone of influence, but otherwise I wouldn't worry about any blow back. Anyone that knows that guy knows how he is."

"Ok . Ok. Alright. Fhnnn."

"Look, take a seat." Carter wobbles his head yes-no before he plops down on the couch next to me. "Breath easy. Everything's alright. Here," I say and toss him the remote. "Find us something to watch."

He finds Saving Private Ryan. "I love this movie. All that trouble just to save Matt Damon, but he is a beautiful man."

Eventually, Carter falls asleep on the couch, but I'm too restless to call it a night. I sit at my desk and prepare for tomorrow's meeting by the lamplight. Tomorrow I'm meeting with Professor Kimball Catchello of Howard University. Specialty: Ancient

History. Latest publication: *Why Man Needed God 10,000 Year Ago and Why He Needs to Forget Him Today.*

Sheez these guys sure are morbid. I'm beginning to become concerned by the lack of divergence of thought on what is such an opinionated matter. I mean is this what these guys spend their time teaching their students? What utility do they expect to derive from all their anti-proselytizing? I mean how are these allegedly educated people able to accept so many other abstract ideas, yet be so bothered by how so many people make sense of the world around them? If they hate what they consider to be superstition so badly, then why don't they spend their time engaged in the positive pursuits of science? I mean, I guess history is an art not a science. But why this emphasis on attacking religion? I mean in my experience churches form communities of people who come together to pray for the suffering, sing hymnals to praise the Lord, consider sacrifice for their fellow man and care for those who are unable to care for themselves. I just have a difficult time comprehending what's so sinister about all that. I mean I recognize that the Christian moral code or the moral code of the world's other established religions may not always jibe with the fleeting social trends of this instant, but is that really a sufficient reason to discard the prescribed behavioral codes of conduct that have sustained mankind's existence and progress throughout the millennia? Can't these *sophisticated* individuals just practice a modicum of tolerance and co-exist?

Then there is the depressing knowledge that I'm now a couple of weeks in to this case, and I still haven't any more insight in to the whereabouts of Finkel's missing manuscript than the day the case was handed to me, or whether it even exists at all. On blind faith and the security of $500 a day, I'll continue to conduct my due diligence.

Chapter 10

After cooking myself up some fried eggs, bacon, banana pancakes, toast and OJ I hop a mid-afternoon taxi to Howard University. Here, the history department is settled in a small unassuming house-like structure. Professor Catchello's office is located on the first right passed the front door. The door stands wide open, but when I peek in it doesn't appear anyone is there. Rather than intrude by presumptively inviting myself to wait inside his office as I did at my Kasowski appointment, I just linger awkwardly around the hallway. Several minutes later a group enters through a door on the opposite side of the hallway. As they draw closer I'm able to discern a professor encircled by a group of adoring students. The professor sees me standing near his office, gives me the once over, and must have put two and two together.

"Mr. Wainwright?"

"Professor Catchello," I say, extending my open palm towards him. We shake hands. He has a jovial smile spread across his face.

"Thank you all for taking me to lunch. I thoroughly enjoyed myself, but for now it's back to work. Hopefully, I'll see you all at the review session tomorrow," Catchello addresses his students before placing a hand on my shoulder and inviting me in to his office with a gesture. "Take a seat," he says as he sits at his desk with his back facing a large window. "Let's see here, Counselor Wainwright," Catchello says as he reads from a page. "Certified Fraud Examiner. Three years at the FDIC. Georgetown Law and Undergrad. Currently, private practice. You became a licensed Private Investigator eight months ago. Concealed weapons permit."

He looks up from the file. "Those permits are rather difficult to come by in the District, aren't they?"

"I had to pull a few strings."

"Are you carrying right now?"

"No. I actually don't own a gun." I lie. I actually bought an unregistered pistol at a Flea Market. There is no record of either the transaction or my possession of it, and I prefer to keep it that way.

"Why get the license if you intended not to use it?"

"In DC, certified fraud examiners are required to also register as private eyes. Most private eyes apply for concealed weapons permits, but I've never worked a job that required I carry a pistol, so I never bought one."

"I see."

"You ask a lot of questions."

"Information puts me at ease. In life, most of us only fear two things: the irrational and the unknown. I'm always rational, so I have only one thing to fear."

"You do seem easy going."

"But it won't last long unless you tell me why you're here."

"I'm looking for contacts and information for a biography I've been assigned to write on the life of the late Dr. Alberto Finkel."

Catchello's lips curl upwards in to an almost snarl. "Finkel and I spoke often." I lean forward in my seat. Catchello is more promising than anyone yet. "Or perhaps it's more accurate to say that we argued frequently," he continues. "You see, Finkel was a historical positivist, whereas my scholarship is far more informed by critical theory."

"So would it be fair to say that your world views were at odds?"

"Finkel's views were frequently at odds with conventional academia. Yet much to my anguish he and his work were well-received by the literate public. The man just wouldn't fall in line. Academic treason, really."

"It sounds to me like you're accusing him of being a free thinker."

Catchello scoffs. "That man and his Judaism. Arch defender of the Abrahamic religions. I swear to see the man breathing was to hear him whispering prayers of apology for Christ's murder."

"Finkel's religion clearly troubles you."

"Of course it does! That a man of academia, and a high standing one at that should be a champion of organized religion. It is sickening to the intellect."

"What bothers you so terribly about another man's religion? Why not just co-exist?"

"The Abrahamic religions uphold the reigning immutable moral code. Morality may be a preservative measure for the general populace, it may be a process of uniting its dispersed members, but it is also used as an agent in the production of the man who is a tool."

"You quote Nietzsche."

Catchello leans back against his chair, reveals an inch of a smile and generally relaxes his demeanor. "So you've read Nietzsche. Very good," he says. Apparently he has relaxed now that he believes my views align with his own, and that I have merely been playing devil's advocate up to this point. He'd best prepare for a rude awakening.

"The Christian moral code has allowed for the preservation of the torch of intelligence for the intervening 2000 years. Nietzsche may have thought that the Superman should ignore the moral code obeyed by the majority of the populace, but what if every person reads Nietzsche and each deems his or herself a Superman? Social harmony would collapse, driving each person's behavior to its meanest, lowest, and most primitive form. Nietzsche living in the world he would create is quickly devoured in the woods. Modern society is allowed to function because we have expectations of our fellow man's behavior. Of course, in extraordinary circumstances an otherwise virtuous man's behavior may depart from the prescribed code, but only for just cause," I say.

"You really believe we should live our lives according to the dictates of an ancient moral code? In light of the science and progress of the ages, what purpose, what utility has it got? *God is Dead!*"

"We live by an ancient moral code because it sustains us; because it works. It's funny you use that hackneyed old Nietzsche quote."

"Why is it funny to you?"

"Because it's a negative affirmation, 'God is dead.' It's funny because you use it to mean God isn't real, but pick apart your chosen logical structure: God is dead. It's logical precedent is "God lived" or "God lived and created man, but no longer uses divine intervention. Nietzsche's syntax reveals an implicit affirmation of the existence of God at some point in history. However, given both our limited knowledge of both science and the human subconscious, among other physically unexplored phenomena, God may still exercise a subtle form of divine intervention beyond the capability of human perception."

"You miss my point, Mr. Wainwright, but perhaps you'll be able to follow this one: We have the opportunity to free ourselves from the prejudiced chains of our ancestors' superstition!"

"For a historian you seem to fail to have a firm understanding of the outcome of social revolution."

"And why's that?"

"Chaos, followed by suffering, followed by a gradual and painful reinstitution of the former status quo. True, new people may be in charge, but the old law is resurrected following the revolution."

"Your conclusion isn't a necessary outcome."

"Actually, I'm afraid it is. You can tinker with the moral fabric of society, but restitch too much too quickly and the preservative quality of that protective blanket will tear, and I promise you that an urban history professor such as yourself is laughably unequipped to survive in such a world."

"Ha-ha. It's you and the Christian dogs who will suffer in the coming world."

"Listen, I'm no tenured professor. I'm just calling them like I see them. I'm not particularly devout myself, but I don't understand all your hostility. It's like your suffering from some neurosis triggered by herd behavior and too much free time. You've let your mind wander down perverted paths."

Catchello slams his fists down on the desk. "Get out! You insult me in my own office! You racist bigot!"

"Racist bigot? For what? Harboring sincerely held beliefs that differ from your own? So much for the freedom to hold divergent opinions," I say.

"No one gives you the right to voice stupidity."

I just look at him and smile before turning and leaving his office. I don't give him the gratitude of hearing me verbalize my final thoughts on him. I wouldn't lower myself to his level. Instead of hailing a cab outside of the University, I decide to walk and think. These history professors around town are testy, opinionated things. And they all seem to have convergent opinions, which in turn seems to fuel their certainty. I guess if there is nothing to change then there is limited need for the social scientist, so they attempt to establish their worth by proclaiming flaws in the social order and then offering their *expert* services to mend the problem. Listen to what they explicitly argue for; they're actually perpetually trying to justify their station in life. Unlike many, it isn't money or goodwill that motivates them: it's power. They long to become the Washington, Adams or Jefferson of the next epic, to stand up and say "it was my idea that set you all free." (It is my idea that you all espouse and follow. It is the limitation of the power of my idea that will frustrate you during the reign of the next paradigm).

I'm restless when I get home. I've nothing really to prepare for tomorrow's meeting with the estranged Mrs. Finkel *if* the purpose of our appointment is to simply lend me some of Al Finkel's journals. Without much more to give my attention, my thoughts drift towards Regina Damasio. I decide to fire her off a quick email.

Regina,

Hope this email finds you doing well. Might you have some time available to chat this afternoon?
best,
Wylie

I make myself a sandwich and saunter around my steaming apartment. Munching away on my ham and cheese, I shoot another email to my apartment manager pleading for some sort of air conditioning relief. After all, I've suffered through this already for a majority of the summer. As I send out the email to my property manager, I receive a reply from Regina.

Hello Wylie!

Sure. I'm actually at the Starbucks on Wisconsin across the street from Safeway grading papers. Ugh. Feel free to stop by!
Regina

Nice. I finish up my sandwich, drop my I-pad in my bookbag and head out the door. Regina's only a couple of blocks away. Despite the last few days' heat of mild intensity, today I'm reminded of what the DC heat can do to a pedestrian. By the time I'm inside the Starbuck's AC zone, I'm totally wilted. Sweat stains everywhere. I spot Regina sitting at a table alone, her earphones in as she stares at a computer screen. She's slightly startled when I take the seat opposite her.

"Wylie," she gasps, and catches her breath.

"Sorry if I snuck up on you."

"No, it's ok. I was just kinda lost in this article I'm reading. I've been totally procrastinating on grading these papers. It's hard to get motivated to read twenty-eight versions of the same paper of varying quality."

"I can only imagine."

"So what's up with you?" she asks. She somewhat startles and excites me when she briefly touches my palm as she's asking her question.

"Not much more than what I was doing when we last spoke. I've been running around town interviewing Professor Finkel's various counterparts at all the different colleges, immersing myself in the literature, trying to hone in on a more accurate picture of the man."

"And what have you found?"

"These local professor's have some jealousy issues."

"Ha. Al was the top of his field. He got to do what he loved *and* make money at it. In certain circles, I've even heard his work described as 'iconic.' It's really difficult to enjoy that much success in the realm of history scholarship."

"These professors I spoke with, they all seemed to harbor a feeling that his ideas often diverged from the mainstream of academic thought. What can you tell me about that?"

"Hm," she guffaws. "I guess you could tie that sentiment back in to their jealousy. Al *was* mainstream historical interpretation. I'd never thought of it before, but come to think of it it does seem like there was a coalition of these guys to try to subvert, refute, or undermine his work. Of course, those guys were usually received as the minority opinion. But now with Al gone. . ."

"Who are those guys?"

"Mostly that lousy American Historical Association."

"Why do you call them lousy?"

"Well they weren't always. It used to be an important forum for historians to meet and discuss their work. But now it's so damned exclusive; it's totally shed its old democratic roots. It's elitist. I mean it's sickening. I'm new to the game, but I've heard a lot of older historians express a lot of disgust with it. If you want to know more, you should really talk to one of them."

"Who should I start with?"

"Um, you might start with Raul Aquino at UVA. You can drop my name, he was my undergrad advisor. I'm sure he would speak with you. I know he's an outspoken critic of the modern permutation of the AHA."

"Raul Aquino. Great thanks I will talk with him."

"Shit," she says as her attention returns to her computer screen.

"What is it?"

"The House just passed legislation to expand the breadth of the 13th Amendment."

"What's your take on all this?"

"I mean, it's a blatant attempt to implement an inept form of communism under the guise of expanding individual liberties."

"What liberties are going to be expanded?"

"First, all debt obligations are declared null-n-void. Second, if you want to quit your job and take up any whimsically unproductive profession, then the government will subsidize your work, which is subject to an automatic approval process, and pay you a middle-class income to be adjusted every year for inflation," she says.

"That's insane. If that takes affect it will disassemble our economic system overnight. We'll be bankrupt in a day. The social order will be destroyed. I mean how are they able to do this?"

"I don't know, it's like popular sentiment just took a crazy turn overnight."

"There has been a sudden, deep shift. That's for sure."

We both sit there silent for a moment, mulling over a fire that has been ignited and risks destroying the entire forest before its dangerous nature is fully understood. I determine to rest these troubling thoughts, and shift my mind somewhere else, somewhere more pleasant. Like by thinking about how attractive Regina can be even when she is dressed down in an old-faded Georgetown t-shirt and lulemon pants, if you can even really call them pants. Her silky brown hair is pulled back in to a ponytail, allowing me to explore the exquisite contours of her cheekbones. Her tight t-shirt reveals her trim figure. Even her commoner's digs can't disguise her natural aristocracy. She's clearly brilliant and if I was still the hopeless romantic of my youth I would be in love, but Angie's absence has left my heart in a current state of disrepair.

"Ugh," Regina emits a disgruntled sigh. "I've been here for two hours and have only managed to grade three papers. At this rate, it will take me the rest of the week to finish. Say, do you want to get out of here?"

"I've been planning my final flight from the city for quite some time."

"Ha-ha. Funny bonehead. No, I mean let's go do something fun. Once I feel guilty for having shirked too much work to have fun, it'll be easier for me to sit down and grade these papers."

"Ok," I say with an involuntary eye roll.

"Hey, I'm not crazy! I'm just mature enough to know how I operate, and I know that guilt really motivates my work ethic."

"What do you propose we do?" I ask.

"Um," she hums as she quickly stows her laptop and students' papers away in her backpack. "Let's either rent bikes or rent bikes and get on the Metro."

"Let's bike to the Metro. It's too hot to bike around for an extended period today."

Regina smiles at my complacency and off we go, up Wisconsin to the intersection of Calvert, where we rent bikes. We peddle up hill a little further before the super-avenue plateaus, and we're both able to peddle forward with ease towards the Tenleytown Station. We lock up our bikes and descend in to the caverns of public transportation. Even today, the monumental multi-

105

story escalators that deliver us below the earth's crust leave me awestruck. After waiting a few playful moments at the subterranean train station, we board a train toward an undecided destination. Only one pair of seats is open on our car, so we sit cozily next to one another. Regina begins telling me about her childhood in eastern Tennessee, about growing up in Knoxville, where football *is* the principle export and sustenance crop of the region. She tells me about studying abroad in Paris during undergrad, about how visiting Versailles, the Louvre, the Eiffel Tower and the many avant garde art districts inspired her to seek a life in an ultra-modern setting, only she desired somewhere they speak her native English. Washington, it seems, satisfies her requirements.

I suggest we disembark at DuPont for all her talk of Paris, but she says no, that DuPont is too obvious. Ultimately, we reemerge on the streets of DC on Farragut Square, in the orbit of George Washington University and the World Bank. My stomach begins to groan for lunch, my sandwich is no longer holding me, so we find some nearby gourmet food trucks. She has the fried chicken and waffles, while I pick up some chicken tikka masala tacos. Eating on a bench, we giggle at the pantomime who's pretending to be a traffic cop at the crosswalk. Once, a car blows its horn at the clown's lack of authority, at which point he begins doing push-ups in the middle of the street. Following a period of carefree wander, in a moment I would describe as happiness, Regina decides to get real and begin probing the complexities and shortcomings of my character. She begins by hurling a question in to the most sensitive domain of my current situation.

"So what's your dating situation? Do you have a girlfriend?"

Just like that, she manages to activate all of my feelings of self-loathing, doubt, and mild depression. I mean, I don't even have the wherewithal to lie.

"I recently got out of a serious relationship."

"Oh, I'm sorry. I didn't mean to *pry.*"

"It's ok."

"How long did you date?"

"About six years."

"Oh my God that's horrible. Did this happen recently?"

"Yeah, like a month or so ago."

"Oh, well then it wasn't exactly yesterday or anything."

"No."

"When is the last time you talked?"

I remember Angie walking in on naked Penelope, Mrs. Finkel was all frazzled, and Angie giving me the shittiest look imaginable, then walking away. "I saw her once like a week ago, but we didn't talk. We haven't talked since we broke up a month or two ago."

"I see. Well, at least you're on the other side of recovery. They say what, a month to recover for each year you were together?"

"I sincerely hope *they* are wrong."

"Have you been dating any?"

"I went on a couple of dates with one girl. Nothing too serious. I'm not trying to jump in to another serious relationship just yet."

"No, no. Of course not."

We both stare at a homeless guy feeding some pigeons in an awkward moment of silence. It's kind of the poor bum to care for the pigeons when he can barely care for himself.

"What about you? Are you dating?" I don't quite finish my sentence when Regina interrupts me.

"No. Heavens no. The doctoral program at Georgetown is no joke. Most days are in at nine every morning, out at eleven every evening."

"Do you ever feel like you work is too hard?"

"Always."

"Then why do you do it? Or *how* do you do it?"

"It's my calling. It's my purpose in life," she says and there is a pause in our conversation. "Why do you write biography?"

"For the crudest reasons," I say, projecting my reasons for being a CFE and PI on to book writing. "To keep myself up. Get paid. Unfortunately, I'm at a place where I'm not really certain why I do what I do, other than earn my wages."

"This breakup has been really hard on you, hasn't it?"

Everything inside of me wants to take a pass on this question, but I begin speaking against my own volition. "I mean we dated since law school. For years, I was either working or spending time with Angie. By the time we broke up, I had only really maintained one other solid friendship in my life, with my friend Carter. And he's a wild man; I can hardly keep up."

"Maybe what we both need is a sort of social renaissance, to channel our inner twenty-one year old."

"That's really not a bad idea. I actually feel like I've been trying to do a little of that lately, without having actually put that solid of a name on it."

"That's great. Maybe you'll have some pointers to teach me."

"I'm afraid I haven't come along very far."

"But I bet you have. You strike me as the modest type."

"It's not difficult to be modest when you've got nothing to brag about."

Regina leans in and kisses me. I think she means to give me a more platonic kiss on the cheek, but when my peripherals detect her leaning in, I turn my head and our lips meet. There's a rather tenacious lashing of the tongues during the approximate five or so seconds the kiss lasts. When its over, she leans back and touches her fingers to her lips.

"I guess there's a little magic left in us both after all," she says. Then she stands and begins to gather her things.

"Where are you going?" I ask, wondering whether I've adequately concealed my desperation. Regina's face is swollen pink with blush. She tries to withhold her smile, but can't help but let it beam through.

"I have a guilty conscience now," she says in an almost laugh and starts to run away.

"Did that just happen because I'm sad?" I stand and call out to her.

"It's because you don't realize how happy you really are," she retorts from a distance, before disappearing in to a dense crowd. When I sit back down, my lips spark a tingling sensation that spreads across my face to my scalp.

Maybe I am happy. There have been two girls now since Angie and I split, if I liberally construe that kiss as an encounter. But of course it was! What else is a kiss? Regina's right. I *am* happy and that's precisely why we had fun today and ended up inadvertently kissing. It's of limited consequence that the kiss was accidental; it was her reaction that said it all.

After soaking up as much of the moment on that bench as possible, I finally begin walking in the general direction towards home. Despite the more romantic alternative forms of transportation available, I hop on the number thirty-one bus northbound. It isn't sexy, but it is *relatively* clean and effective. At least the bus is cleaner than a large fraction of the taxis in this city. At home, I drop on the couch in front of the TV. I feel my sweat-covered skin sticking to my couch's leather fabric, so I email my landlord to further inquire about when the AC problem will be fixed. To my surprise, she emails me back a few moments later. "Soon. Hopefully by tomorrow evening. Thanks for your patience." Tomorrow doesn't seem like a terrible amount of time to wait for the end of a seemingly never-ending problem.

Now I'm taken a little off guard to see a familiar face being introduced on the TV screen. Professor Anthony Silviano. I turn up the volume.

"Professor Silviano is distinguished Professor of World History visiting us from just across town at George Washington University. Professor Silviano we've invited you on to the program tonight to elicit your views on the proposed Constitutional Amendment that would expand the protections of the 13th Amendment. Would you like to introduce us to your thoughts on the matter?" the TV host asks.

"Yes, first I'd like to thank you Bob and the network for inviting me here tonight," Silviano says.

"Certainly," Bob Weinghart says.

"Any discussion of the expansion of the 13th Amendment would need to begin with a historical understanding of the original Amendment, which was adopted in 1865. What the 13th Amendment did was grant African-American slaves their freedom, or in other words it nullified the slave owner's property rights to his slave property. For the first time in American History since European settlement the law now says "no man may own another man." Of course, there were many complex factors that led to the fighting of the Civil War, but slavery was basically the linchpin of animosity during the Civil War era," Silviano says.

"Of course, in the immediate wake of the enactment of the 13th Amendment," Silviano continues, "scholars set to work, furiously searching for ways to maintain the social order. In the post-slave era, the elite's control over their labor would never again enjoy as firm a grip as before; however, with careful maneuvering they could basically recreate much of the society that existed in Antebellum South. In a capitalist system, a free economic agent needs sustenance to survive. One could farm, but farming requires land as well as a breadth of skills. We were, of course, moving forward in to a post-agrarian society. So in a burgeoning economy of specialists, one needs *money* to survive. We see a rapid rise in the monetization of the American economy during the decades to follow the conclusion of the Civil War. There was the failed Reconstruction effort to provide every slave with "forty acres and a mule." There was the codification of the Jim Crow laws. There were increasingly only two ways for a person to care for him or herself: work and earn wages; or borrow money, go in to debt, and then work to both sustain yourself and pay down your borrowed money. The catch: the average person could not get what they wanted *unless* they went in to debt. Want a house? Go in to debt. Want a horse? Go in to debt. Although the laborers in this new economy were not the property of the elites, they still worked for the benefit of the elites, which is the entirety of what the elites sought all along. The new law prohibited ownership by one human being of another, so that a *leasing arrangement* between one human and another became

111

a social norm. Another man's entire lifetime of beneficial labor can even be leased, so long as it is not owned," Silviano says.

"But we have to work to live," the host interjects.

"We have to *care* for ourselves to live, but we don't have to work for others to live. It is sufficient to work for others to live, but it is not necessary. Modern capitalist cultural and technological gifts have enamored the majority of society beyond the point of even questioning whether there might be a better, more superior way of living. People work to buy consumer goods, but what they're really purchasing behind the expensive shoes, sunglasses, cars, or sneakers, is a glimmer of sovereignty, or class. In fact, when they spend those dollars for freedom they are actually reinforcing their own bondage. I blame this on the original lie—religion," Silviano says.

"Well this is interesting. I hope you'll elaborate on your critique of religion?"

"First off, those who believe in religion don't question its guiding virtues, specifically the Christian work ethic. Why is it *ethical* that we should always work? I believe that we have reached a point today where there is not enough necessary work to go around. Why should an individual feel compelled to toil their precious few days away on Earth in the pursuit of work as an end in and of itself? I say if you don't have anything productive to do, then enjoy yourself. Enjoy life. But this will not be possible until religion is destroyed. And no, I'm not talking about merely undermining its central tenets. What I'm advocating is a clean break from religion, burning its books, toppling its buildings, wiping it forever from both the human conscious and subconscious so that *science* may reign as king and . . ."

I have to turn the TV off. Silviano is turning out to be a militant lunatic. So much for tolerance. So much for co-existence. So much for the humanity and faith religion has provided us with over the millennia. These egomaniacal professors are so desperate to be thought of as the most intelligent beings in the Universe that they sophistically kill God, discount the existence of Intelligent life in the Universe beyond Earth's atmosphere, and basically ignore fundamental facts of reality so they may exalt themselves as gods. But enough of that pedagogical bullshit.

I run downstairs to Breadsoda for a sandwich and a PBR. Breadsoda on a weekday is a bastion of hipster counterculture in an otherwise sea of Capitol City conformity. It's now the 16th day of July. I'm supposed to receive a pretty substantial payment for my work from Pioneer Press this Friday. I guess that probably means I should start working on a rosy-colored summary of my work since I last talked to Lulu. After I pay the bill, I quietly walk back upstairs to my apartment with a happy mind filled with thoughts of Regina, and our kiss. Maybe it was an event that would only occur in that single moment in time, but I still have every right to savor it.

Chapter 11

I have a lot of anxiety this morning in anticipation of my meeting with Mrs. Finkel. No doubt, the blue hair is an important character interview and Finkel's journals may provide some key insight in to his methods. What was his process for writing manuscripts? Who did he confide in or bounce ideas off of, if anyone, during the incubation stages? Only due diligence, access to proper resources, and time can answer these questions. I also need to make contact with Professor Raul Aquino of UVA. Sitting at my desk, I open my email account.

Dear Professor Raul Aquino,

I hope this email finds you doing well. My name is Wylie Wainwright, a biographer under contract with Pioneer Publishing to write about the late distinguished Professor Al Finkel. Might I meet with you sometime in the near future to discuss your perspective of his work's legacy? I would be deeply indebted.

best regards,

Wylie Wainwright

After I send the email, I start grooming and laying out clothes for my afternoon appointment. I'm certain my exploits have already left Mrs. Finkel with quite an impression, so I figure I could use the added power of a suit. I nick myself shaving and begin to wonder whether the blood will ever stop. I eat some frosted flakes along with sliced banana. Staring in the mirror, I remove the tissue paper from my shaving cut only to have the blood begin trickling out once more. I can't put on my white button-down shirt until my face stops bleeding. Time starts to get away from me as I procrastinate with purpose. I eventually concede and put an unnecessarily large Band-Aid over the cut and across a wide region of my face. The Band-Aid is awkward between my lower lip and chin, but at least it holds in the bleeding. Then I dress quickly, buttoning my shirt and, due to time constraints, force myself to find satisfaction with a half-Windsor knot.

I'm meeting Mrs. Finkel at the Four Season's restaurant on M Street, a conspicuously overpriced establishment called Bourbon Steak. I wonder which marketing firm came up with that lousy name. I see Mrs. Finkel sitting at a table in the middle of the restaurant before I even reach the host's stand.

"Hello sir," the host says. "One for lunch?"

"No, I'm actually meeting someone," I say and point to Mrs. Finkel's table. The host seems to examine me, as if to wonder whether I'm a family relation or in pursuit of an indecent proposal. He must not have made up his mind by the time we arrive at the table because his emotions do not betray him.

"Enjoy your lunch," he says with a slight bow before returning to his podium near the restaurant's entrance.

Mrs. Finkel and I exchange the usual cordialities. Our waiter arrives and takes our orders. I can sense Mrs. Finkel is waiting for some privacy from the service before we begin our business.

"I'll have those orders up shortly," the waiter says as he closes his black leather notebook and leaves us to ourselves.

"Before you get too nervous, just relax because I have the journals with me," she says, patting her oversized old-ladies purse. "Reading these should give you some insight in to Al without all of his customary layers of smoke. He was a complex man, but all of it was for a purpose. Sure, he spent a lot of time in his study, but he was no social apathetic. No, his real talent lie in understanding

115

people. That's why his writing was so popular: he utilized pre-existing channels to disseminate his ideas. The grunt work, which he spent most of his life engaged in, was research," Mrs. Finkel says as she intermittently butters and chews on a roll.

"So he could read people and understand his audience?"

"That's correct. My earnest respect for his professional career is why I tell you this now. Because I need to understand your intentions before I provide you with any more assistance in your endeavor," Mrs. Finkel says.

"Isn't an accurate portrayal the goal of every biography?"

"I won't provide any assistance if you intend to slander or defame Al. We ultimately had our relationship problems, but I still admire and respect his career and what his work stands for. Few others in this world have as much integrity as Al Finkel. His honesty is what made his career. Unfortunately, it was his honesty that also ruined our marriage."

"I see."

"This being said, I expect that you would keep your discussion of his private life to a minimum. I turn over these journals to you in confidence, so you may better understand him, but I'm not giving these to you to be exploited. This is why I'm asking you to sign this agreement drafted by my attorney. It gives me the right to editorial censorship of anything you write about Al. You will avail yourself of negative injunctions. Otherwise, Al's journals will be left in a safety deposit box to be forgotten by time," Mrs. Finkel says. She slides a simple yet airtight agreement to me from across the table. Clearly, it's easy for me to sign this document since the whole biography story is a scam.

"There you go," I say after signing the agreement. Mrs. Finkel takes a moment to scrutinize my signature. Satisfied, she takes four leather-bound journals from her purse and places them on the table for my taking. "These should be immensely useful for my work. Thank you. And trust me, I will respect your late husband's memory."

"What will you say about me?"

"What would you like to have said about you?" Perhaps you would even like to pen the chapter on your relationship with Al? Have in print what you want in print, save me some work. Everyone wins," I say.

"Well, that is a flattering suggestion, but I've never written anything."

"Oh," I say with a wave of my hand, "don't even worry about that. You write whatever you want to write as raw as you want to give it to me, and I'll handle the editing and polishing. It is, after all, what I do professionally."

"Hm, that is certainly a thought I will consider. May I take some time to think it over?"

"You certainly may."

Mrs. Finkel strums her fingers across the table, contemplating. "What if what I write isn't accurate? What if it over romanticizes my role in Al's life?"

"Now Mrs. Finkel, having spoken with you today, I'm certain you wouldn't do that," I say. Mrs. Finkel fingers her hairspray-stiffened hair, flattered by my presumption of her honesty. While she's still speechless, no doubt already writing her chapter in her head, the waiter arrives with our entrees. For Mrs. Finkel, scallops and vegetable medley. For me, grilled chicken Caesar salad. Every so often, Mrs. Finkel looks up from eating and smiles at me, once with multi-colored vegetables in her teeth.

"I really should tell you this," Mrs. Finkel breaks the silence halfway through finishing her entre.

"Tell me what Mrs. Finkel?"

"I'm just afraid if I don't tell you now, that you may learn of it anyway in his journals. I haven't read them myself."

"What is it Mrs. Finkel?" I say consolingly, my intuition telling me she's about to reveal an episode of emotional damage. She vacillates, touching her female features: her hair, face, breasts and waist as if someone has just told her she isn't pretty.

"I suspect Al of having an affair. . . with his young research assistant," Mrs. Finkel says. Shamefully, this is a prospect I've scarcely considered, especially since I sparked off an affair with Regina myself. I consider Mrs. Finkel's suspicion. Regina was in a position of trust with Al, and trust is a necessary condition for deceit and betrayal. Plus, Miss Finkel isn't the only person to have insinuated an affair: Professors Silviano and Lockington both floated that speculation as well. Could Regina have caught wind of what I'm up to and be intentionally trying to keep me close? Of course, there are a myriad of possible explanations for Regina and Al to have had a relationship beyond the walls of academia. A simple affair isn't enough to suggest that Regina might have resorted to some sort of jealous foul play *or* have stolen Al's last manuscript.

"What facts lead you to this conclusion, Mrs. Finkel?"

"The opportunist little bitch. The foremost authority on history in the World, and he chooses a 24-year old bimbo to aid him in his research? Come on. He's had fully-tenured professors abandon their positions just to have the opportunity to learn from his methods. A 24-year old gorgeous girl? She was just out of undergrad when he hired her. He was after something other than academic expertise. You tell me, Mr. Wainwright, where did she provide the value in their *professional* relationship?"

"You believe she slept with him to gain the opportunity to work next to him?"

"Perhaps it was no more insidious than that. Maybe she was after his money. Or maybe the insurance policy?"

"What insurance policy?"

"Oh, well when Al and I were first wed he purchased a life insurance policy on himself, so in case anything ever happened I would be taken care of. The matter of the policy was never brought up in our property separation agreement, and as far as I know he always maintained it with me as the beneficiary. Well, over the years it grew to be a very lucrative prospect for me, but I had no control over it. Ultimately, I received the windfall, so maybe the little bitch didn't have her hooks as deep in him as I had thought after all."

But maybe you did, Mrs. Finkel. But you didn't have a clear motive for stealing the manuscript, if it ever existed. Regina, however, does have a motive I hadn't considered. If Al *had* written a secret manuscript, then if anyone knew anything about it that person would have been Regina. Regina might have taken the manuscript to later publish it under her own name. One thing is clear: I need to determine whether or not that manuscript ever existed. That's what I'm being paid to chase, and all other facts can be built on the affirmation or negation of this fundamental question.

After we finish our meal, we both refuse dessert. Mrs. Finkel insists on paying the bill. I put up token resistance, insisting I pay for the bill. When Mrs. Finkel's change arrives, we shake hands and part company.

Standing on the street outside of the Four Seasons, I'm troubled by an innate flaw in Washington, DC: there is terrifically little to do on a day like today in a buttoned-up city like Washington. First, there really aren't any pools. Second, my apartment doesn't have AC. Third, everyone works during the day. It's boring to be an entrepreneur in a city without a leisure class. Even those supported by trust funds are busy with some all-consuming activity, like grassroots political movements and stalking politicians. Relaxation here is impossible. Overpopulation and expense are the two primary factors that leads to a culture of both stress and pettiness. To find evidence of my claim, I have to look no further than myself. So overwhelmed by the lack of mid-afternoon recreation am I that I decide to do some work.

I hop a cab up Wisconsin Avenue to the Georgetown Public Library. Recently renovated, I'm comfortable sitting at my large table facing a window overlooking Georgetown, Rosslyn, and the Potomac River. Al Finkel's personal journals are the subject of my interest. Several hours and halfway through his first journal, I'm both stimulated and perplexed by Al's complex and at times seemingly convoluted understanding of the world around him. Of course, he wrote these journals for an audience of one, presumably to arouse his own recollection and not to provide an objective account of his life and times for others. I begin to wonder how many verifiable revelations this man had which he never shared with anyone. I earmark my place when a librarian announces five minutes until closing over the PA system. As I saunter along the sidewalk I ponder about Al Finkel: no doubt he was a man of some genius, but what information escapes me? Am I even one iteration closer to concluding this case than I was on day one?

Chapter 12

Since my meeting with Mrs. Finkel, I have locked myself away in my apartment, reading Al's journals as well as the works of his contemporaries with a focus on religion. Unfortunately, Al's journals pre-date the period he might have worked on the alleged missing manuscript. He certainly had a number of ideas for future books, though. The man was a champion of the brainstorm.

As for his *peers*, they all seem to be concerned with the notion of the villainy of religion. Eradicate it. Root it out. Show the religious sentiment no quarter. Tolerance is tantamount to acquiescence, and acquiescence is tacit approval. Meanwhile, talking heads are on television attacking religion on all fronts. "Remove 'In God We Trust' from the currency." "Repeal rights to give prayers before public meetings." "Immediately cease making accommodation for others' sincerely held religious beliefs." "God is Dead." "Dawkins for President." It's honestly difficult for me to watch the unthinking herd gang up on the turn-the-other-cheek crowd. It's like compassion itself has been indicted. When asked who they worship they say: "Government," "myself," or "nothing." When asked what new laws would be implemented if all laws founded in Christian morality were overturned, there is zero consensus. Some with exotic sexual predispositions insist all limits on marriage should be repealed to allow bigamy, polygamy, incest, bestiality, or any other relationship that can be conjured. A loose alliance of militia and MMA fighters argue for the repeal of assault and battery laws, as well as murder laws. Swift-talking businessmen seek to have the Securities Exchange Commission disbanded, as well as common law fraud rules and other laws that have found their friends in jail. Media outlets of all varieties seek to have defamation, slander, and libel laws rolled back. Counterfeiters cry for an end to Intellectual Property law.

The most vocal movement, of course, is for the expansion of the 13th Amendment to abolish money lending of all varieties, making all labor contracts voidable for the benefit of the employee, as well as vastly expanding social entitlement programs. For the first time in World History, 13th Amendment proponents argue, everyone in America will be entitled to a living wage without the expectation of a modicum of work in return.

I've been reading these history books and watching the political news all day. In the financial news, the stock market is already off several thousand points in anticipation of the market's fears of a complete government takeover of the world's free markets. Millions are protesting in the streets. I feel like this situation is only one more straw away from erupting in to full-scale riots.

Then I receive an email. It's from Professor Raul Aquino. He apologizes for the late notice, but he can meet me today if I care to drive all the way out to Charlottesville. He adds a time constraint: "I'm leaving the country soon for my native central America if this political situation deteriorates any further. Given my current environment, I fear I have no other choice."

"I'll leave immediately," reads my reply to Professor Aquino's invitation to meet.

I quickly get dressed and walk out the front of my building. People are screaming, chanting, and carrying signs with upside down crosses, among other causes. Cuss words spew from the demonstrator's mouths. Nervous taxis and other motorists lay on their horns and maneuver around protestors who stand in the streets.

Two masked men throw a brick through the window of the furniture store below my apartment building, and I begin to run. I start the ignition and accelerate, across Wisconsin and on to the neighborhood roads of Georgetown. I pass brawls, burglaries, and at-odds demonstrations that I'm more than glad not to be a part of. I resolve not to stop my vehicle until I'm a safe distance away from this city of political unrest. Key Bridge is surprisingly clear, but at least one building on M Street is engulfed in flames. As I speed away on I-395, I don't look back.

I've only visited Charlottesville once, several years back during my undergrad years, for a football game. It's charming country with astute architecture, albeit a particularly WASPy culture of elitist drunken debauchery and Sunday dress clothes. I park my car on Charlottesville's Corner commercial district, filled with shops and bars, adjacent to Mr. Jefferson's Grounds. I stride passed the Rotunda and down the lawn towards New Cabell Hall. All-in-all, Charlottesville and UVA are much quieter than DC, even given the immense strain in the national discourse.

I find Professor Aquino's office on the fourth floor. *He* is not as calm and reflective as the rest of his surroundings.

"Who are you?" he snaps agitatedly.

"Wylie Wainwright. We corresponded via email," I say.

"Right," he says. Some of the stress in his shoulders drops, but he's still frantically running around his office. Sitting on his desk are a couple of half-filled moving boxes. He crouches down, opens a large book to an earmarked page, and begins reading.

"I really hate to interrupt what it is your doing sir, but I just drove *all* the way down from Washington for a few moments of your time," I say. He peers up at me from his crouched position, shuts the heavy book with a thud, stands, drops the book in a moving box and leans against the window behind his desk.

"I'll bet you're glad to be out of there. I'll bet DC is a madhouse," he says.

"It is, and I am."

"Do you remember what happened the last time there was even a discussion of rolling property rights of this magnitude?"

"No, I—"

"Civil War. No legislation had even been introduced to either legislative body. Lincoln's election was all it took to spark a civil war. Today we've got legislation that has passed the House and is set to be considered and held to vote in the Senate in the following days. The poly-scis around here say that if it goes to the States, they've likely got the support to pass it. Worse, they won't have to pass it before heated conflict erupts. It's all beginning now. The time to leave with both your health and liquid assets is now. By next week you'll only be able to escape with the clothes on your back. After that. . ."

"As distressing as all this is, I'm actually here to discuss a somewhat unrelated matter. I would like to ask you some questions about your past affiliation with the American Historical Association."

"Those *plague-en-ess* rats," he says without a bit of remorse in his voice. "They undermine the integrity of the entire discipline."

"What do you mean? Were you not once a member of the AHA?"

"I was a member of the Association when it was still a democracy, when it was still a forum of free thinkers. It came to pass that the AHA changed; the men at the top changed the rules through executive action to consolidate their power. First, they manipulated the body of historians by controlling the grants, directing the fields of research to be pursued, controlling the channels of publication and media appearances. They became so powerful that a sharp criticism from one of the titans was equivalent to the burial of a body of work; if not an entire career. Then they stopped holding elections for terms on the executive counsel. They began filling vacancies through appointment. Finally, once they had consolidated so many avenues of influence in the hands of the executive counsel, they turned all of the ordinary members out of the association altogether. It was a silent coup. The ordinary members are gone. Today, the average American's memory of American History has undergone a swift revision, all at the hands of the American Historical Society in pursuit of their political ambitions."

"Why has no one said anything?"

"Our voice has been taken from us, Mr. Wainwright. In order to write a successful history, one needs the seal of approval of the AHA's executive counsel. Without it, a historian is effectively silenced. Without the AHA's approval, there are no book reviews, no TV appearances, no product distribution. They control the information. But because I'm no longer a member of the AHA, I seem like a kook. My opinion, along with the opinions of numerous other historians who refuse to play ball, are dismissed. We've been lucky enough, or at least those of us who have, to keep our teaching jobs."

"Why not go along with them? If for no other reason, than to get in just good enough with them to have your thoughts voiced?"

"Many have tried. The AHA requires strict conformity with their ideology and political agenda. Where there was no drama they've sought to create it. They want to be the vanguard of the next revolution. They want to be immortalized for their role in history, but first they need the canvas of a famously historical moment upon which to paint their eternal memories. They need to create a storm so large that centuries if not millennia will stop what they are doing to pay attention."

"You're telling me there is a conspiracy to control the official interpretation of historical events?"

"Yes, but they didn't start with modern history. They're reinterpreting *all* history in order to influence the events that are happening today. They alter how you think about yesterday, which alters your behavior today, which sets in motion a totally unforeseeable tomorrow. I'm afraid they're playing a masterful game of chess with the human consciousness."

"And you are fleeing the field of battle?"

"That isn't true. I was deceived as were you. No, I'm retrenching in a safe area with some other like-minded individuals until we can strategize a theoretically successful counterattack. I am afraid that to stay here would be to have our best efforts paralyzed."

"And just a few men have been able to perpetrate this entire conspiracy?"

"Silviano, Kasowski, Chandler, Catchello, White and Lockington are at the top of it all. And no. They aren't in this alone; they're only the principals taking care of the history angle. They have cohorts in the floating apex of many pyramids of power. We vaguely know that they act in large part for the promise of eternal fame, yet there is so much scrupulous calculation written in their comings and goings. I'm afraid we don't know how large their conspiracy is, or who is ultimately pulling the strings."

127

The adrenaline is gushing through my veins. Unless this guy is either nuts or playing a cruel joke on me, I've been right in the middle of this thing the entire time. We exchange contact information, I wish him best luck on his travels and leave him to his packing. Sour on the thought of returning to the DC chaos this evening, I rent a hotel room in Charlottesville, so I might relax and try to reconcile these tremendous revelations of thought with one another.

After a cold shower, numerous questions dominate my mental processes: Is Raul Aquino crazy? Jealous of his betters? Overreacting to temporary social instability onset by the proposal of radical changes to Federal law?

Or is he on to something? These historians do seem to share the same bitter fascination with religious resentment; so much goes without even saying. But to claim they're involved in a conspiracy?

I realized I didn't even mention Al Finkel, and we still talked about so much that I've learned over the past few weeks. Am I conflating my case with the national discourse in the news media? Or are there really subtle links between the AHA's ideological dissemination and this legislation to "expand" the 13th Amendment?

I want to meet with Silviano again, but I doubt he cares to meet with me. Feeling aggressive, I email him anyway. Much to my surprise, he responds shortly thereafter that he would be available to meet me for a drink tomorrow at a fancy place downtown called *Conch Reis Oceania*. Lying on the comfortable hotel bed, I don't bother messing around with the TV or reading because I want to get back to DC early before the traffic and protestor chaos begins.

Chapter 13

I sneak back in to DC in the wee hours of the morning. I cross Key Bridge at about 5:45am. It's relieving to find the streets mostly clear, with the exception of a remarkably heavy police presence. I park in my lot and hit the stairs to my apartment. A cool, arctic chill blasts me on my entry. There *is* air conditioning in DC and it *is* amazing. I could kiss my apartment manager. I collapse on my couch as I so often do. My mind wants to race, but it's simply out of fuel. Nothing to be done about it.

I must have fallen asleep because I open my eyes now to see Carter standing over me shaking me violently.

"Fucking stop Carter. You're hurting me," I say. Despite my whiny protest, he continues rocking me, striking me each time in the ribs and abdomen. I feel like he's going to cause bruising. "What?" I scream and sit bolt upright. Blood quickly rushes to my head, and I feel faint. "What," I mutter sheepishly.

"Let's go to the baseball game," Carter says, his eyes lit up like Christmas.

"Mid-week afternoon baseball game? Don't you have work?"

"*At* the baseball game. All sorts of power people taking off for the game today. Nats versus Reds. Everyone's saying it's a preview of the National League Championship game."

"Isn't it too hot for baseball?" I manage to say, drowsily fighting for my right to rest.

"That's why they sling those ice cold beers. They help moderate the temperature. Help you keep your cool."

"I've, Carter, umgh, dude I've got this important meeting tonight."

"Oh yeah?" Carter asks and crosses his arms. "With who?"

"Anthony Silviano. It's for this case I'm working on."

"Man, you're case *is* chasing purple dragons! Besides, didn't you just meet with that clown?"

"A couple of weeks ago."

"What do you expect to learn from him tonight that you didn't already figure out?"

"I—I don't know. Maybe being around him will lead me to the next clue."

"Like what? That you're a lunatic on a wild goose chase looking for a book that never existed?"

" Fuck Carter. Look at you. Are you really comfortable going to such a public spectacle in the middle of all these demonstrations and riots?"

"Are you really trying to arouse my fear of terrorist attacks to keep me from baseball? Listen up Opie: I lived in DC both before and after 9/11 and nothing, no terrorist organization's threats nor my fear of the unknown, nor domestic political instability is going to prevent me from going to that baseball game today."

"Ok man, well sorry if I offended your sense of ordinary day patriotism, but I'm just too tired to go. I'm sorry you don't respect my work, but it's all I got. Maybe this meeting with Silviano will be worthless, but as long as I'm banking $500 a day, I'm going to stay on my feet for Pioneer Publishing. I mean for crissakes I'm trying to build a brand here; I figure if anyone could understand that, then it would be you."

"That's low Wylie. You know how tender I am for the cold-blooded businessman in me. Ok, fine. Rest up and go play detective tonight. Maybe I'll call, well no. Shit Wylie. This city could actually be fun if there were anyone here cool enough to enjoy it."

"Sorry dude."

"Well ain't no thing," Carter says, letting out a deep sigh, as he lumbers across the room towards the door. "But alright dude I'm out."

"Alright. Later man," I say. I hear the door close behind Carter's exit.

Now I'm awake; Carter's stimulated me just enough to prevent me from going back to sleep, so I lay on my couch staring at the ceiling thinking about nothing. Nothing except how fucking old I am. I mean, who turns down an epic baseball game to do optional work when they get paid whether or not they work? Finish the job. Finish. the. job. I believe I have six more days on my current contract. The fifteen grand I have coming in is well needed: it pays my rent for the whole year. Before this job, I was starting to struggle. It's tough running a start-up in an ultra-expensive city. While I've got work, I need to be doing everything I can to justify my expense, especially from the point of view of angling for a contract extension, or at least referrals.

I get up and take a seat at my desk. I've learned a lot about this microcosm of academe lately; however, this is scarcely what I am being paid for. My client wants the results *they* asked for. They want that manuscript; they want the product they paid for.

Later in the evening, I arrive at the restaurant *Conch Reis Oceania*. I don't usually hang around these types of places; pretension permeates the air. From valets wearing red vests to the hostess who I find more attractive than any participant in the latest Sports Illustrated swimsuit edition. Another couple is just ahead of me conversing with the hostess when I arrive, so I fall in to line. The dimly lit bar's centerpiece is a towering rack of illuminated wine bottles perhaps three stories tall. The variously hued bottles fill the tower like an etch-a-sketch. I'm suddenly further amused to watch an acrobat rhythmically climb the tower, retrieve a vintage, and repel back to bar level. Note to self: pass on the wine.

"May I help you?" the hostess asks, the line having dissipated without my noticing.

"Certainly," I say as I make the mistake of looking this girl in the eye. For a moment my once cogent thoughts turn to fog. "Certainly."

"Te-he-he. Well what may I help you with?"

"Oh," I finally recall, "I'm meeting someone for drinks. Anthony Silviano."

The girl glances over her shoulder and peers back in to the dark recesses of the dining room. She seems to pause for a moment as she has a brief internal debate. But then she lifts a drink menu. "Right this way."

We approach who I gradually discern to be Silviano. He's accompanied by another unfamiliar man. Both are dressed in fine suits. Both carry the air of always- serious men trying to relax, but who are unable to release the pint-up tension due to their nature. Silviano jumps to his feet when he sees me; his level of cordiality shocks me. The man sitting opposite Silviano stands and buttons his dark suit jacket. I quickly notice the unknown man is adorning a Congressman's lapel pin. Silviano checks his watch. Then he extends a handshake.

"Wylie I was just about to accuse you of being early, but I see you're just on time. Mr. Wainwright, this is Congressman Edward Callahan, of Connecticut's Second District. The Congressman and I go way back, and we were just catching up on old times."

"That's nice," I say. Everyone sits down. I order a scotch rocks, which is what the other two appear to be having.

"Do yew remember *that* swim meet?"

132

"Eddie, you're never going to stop being proud of this one, are you?"

"Yew," the Congressman starts. He points a finger at Silviano before turning his attention to me. "This un wuz gullible. A naïve 'lil thing. Wes used't be on the swim team together. Anthony finished number one, and I finished number two. *Always*. Until one day I cided it wuz my day to win. What'd I do to beat yew 'atta day Ant?"

"You handcuffed me to a flagpole across campus," Silviano says gruffly.

"'At's right! And I won 'at eight-hundred meter. Yale wins!" the Congressman proclaims in an elevated pitch that carries throughout the restaurant. The Congressman throws back the rest of his scotch in a moment of utter glee. When he slams the glass down, we're all infected with an inexplicable laughter. The Congressman is clearly in a state of excitement. I laugh to be polite. I don't know why Silviano is laughing. The cocktail waitress returns to the table to check-in on us.

"May I get you gentlemen anything else?" she asks.

"Double," the Congressman shouts and slams his glass on the table once more. Silviano chuckles a bit nervously as the waitress records the order on her notepad.

"Same," I say as her attention turns toward me. She makes a brief notation before looking to Silviano.

"I should be alright from here," he says, tapping what remains of his previous scotch with his gold ring baring the engraved letters: "AHA."

She smiles and leaves us.

"Yes I apologize Wylie. The Congressman and I were just having dinner and catching up, and we ended up stewing around

133

longer than we had intended," Silviano says. I gather that his words are intended as more of a censure of the Congressman's behavior than they are an apology to me.

"Really no worries. I don't think anyone in this town has ever frowned at making the acquaintance of a Congressman," I say.

"No, I don't suppose they have," Silviano says.

The waitress returns and drops off our drinks. The Congressman takes a brutish chug from his glass, consuming half of its contents, and puts the glass on the table, and wipes the foam off his lip with his shirtsleeve.

"So what about yew two? How know each other?" the Congressman asks.

"Wylie and I are in related fields," Silviano says.

"O," the Congressman mutters, furrows his brow, and further lowers the scotch level in his glass.

"Wylie is a biographer. He is currently researching a piece on the late Al Finkel," Silviano says.

The Congressman snickers, seemingly at hearing the name Al Finkel.

"What?" I ask.

"Book'll never get out," the Congressman says and laughs maniacally some more. His cheeks are blush from booze and jubilance. Even the dome of his bald head is reddening.

"Which book are you referring to?" I ask.

Silviano is shooting rapid-fire glances between the two of us. "I believe he's referring to the publishing process. To someone unfamiliar with the system, it can seem as though your book will never see print. First, there's all the time spent writing. I once spent two years *after* writing a manuscript, waiting on a publisher to print

134

the thing. It's truly outrageous how long the process can take," Silviano says.

"It'd of been a real mess," the Congressman says. I don't know whether the Congressman's statement was precognition or a self-fulfilling prophecy, but he spills his drink all down his luckily black suit.

"Ok, I hate it, but I'm sending you home," Silviano says, taking the Congressman by the arm and escorting him to the door before they disappear outside. A moment or two later Silviano reappears and coolly takes a seat on his former chair.

"The pressures of public office can be quite demanding. I'm afraid you met the Congressman tonight in a rather run-down state," Silviano says.

"I understand completely," I say.

"Good. Then there's no reason to address the situation further."

"None at all."

"Then where should we steer our conversation from here?" Silviano asks.

But I'm not on the same wavelength with Silviano when he asks his question. I'm pondering the semantics of the Congressman's last two lines: "The book will never get out" and "It'd have been a real mess." The first phrase could have easily been directed towards my faux biography; however, his second phrase was in the past tense. Was the Congressman skewing his grammatical tense due to his relative inebriation, or was he referring to a pre-existing manuscript? Perhaps Al Finkel's missing manuscript? Or am I just a paranoid stoner reading too deeply in to things?

"Sorry," I say following an awkward silence. "I felt so focused when I arrived, but you and your friend are both so *entertaining* that I'm afraid I've lost my train of thought."

"Again, I apologize. But what is it? You came here to discuss a specific point with me?"

"Oh yes, there it is. I'm about to start a sort of generic chapter on the historical research and writing process. I was hoping that when it's completed you might critique it for me pre-publication."

"We can certainly take care of that for you."

"I would be much obliged," I say.

The cocktail waitress returns. "Anything else?"

"Just settle up," Silviano says. He reaches in to his wallet and gives the waitress his credit card. On the card are the emboldened letters 'AHA.'

"I should be finishing a relatively polished draft soon."

"Send it over. It's summer. Professor's do nothing in the summer," Silviano says. I start to offer him some cash for my drinks, but he refuses. He signs his tab, and we exit the restaurant together, parting company on the sidewalk as we each walk our separate ways.

It's late for a weekday when I finally make it back to Georgetown, and I have a burning desire to share what I have learned with Regina. I know it's probably too late to initiate a lengthy conversation with a girl who's got a day job, but I allow my enthusiasm to overcome my hardwired sense of manners.

"Are you awake? Are you available to talk?" I text. I wait and wait, but after an hour I have yet to receive a response. She's probably already asleep, so I try to convince myself.

I load a bowl and sit back to relax, but rather than relax the cannaboids cause my thoughts to race down previously unforeseeable channels. Am I trying to turn a fragment of information, perhaps meaningless in its context, in to a piece of information broad-ranging in its implications with a potential to crack this case?

Silviano's explanation of the Congressman's words easily negates my suspicions, but Silviano's words were his and not the words of the Congressman. Regardless whether the Congressman's drunken utterances are significant to the case or not, they're still enough to give me some hope that the manuscript is out there and that my investigation will turn up more than nothing.

I scurry over to the fridge for a Coca-Cola to help calm my upending weed buzz. Although the sugar soothes my marijuana induced anxiety, the caffeine is an undesirable additional ingredient. Lying on my bed sipping soda, I scroll through all the news articles I've already read earlier today on my i-Pad. I try to watch Netflix, but for some reason my Internet connection isn't strong enough to stream video. A yawn suddenly comes over me, and I lay my coke and i-Pad on the night stand, hoping my physiology will follow my subconscious in to a state of . . .

Chapter 14

"Vhn, vhn. . . vhn vhn." I crack my eyes open to stream my first hazy perception of the new day. My phone is vibrating, and by gauging the amount of light that's seeking refuge in my cave-like room, it is much earlier than the 10am alarm I set on my phone. I flip the phone over. Two new messages from Regina Damasio.

"Sorry I was asleep when you texted."

"I'm glad you texted. I've been doing some research and would really like to share some thoughts with you," Regina's message reads.

"When you free?" I text as I sit up in bed and take a deep, oxygenating breath.

"Now. Come over to my place. 3425 Reservoir," she texts.

I guess the competing emotions I'm now experiencing are what *they* warn about when cautioning against mixing business and pleasure. My thoughts are clouded by the divergence of emotion between my professional connection and my romantic attraction to Regina. I definitely take more time to get cleaned up, shaving a one-day growth of beard and even flossing. Is it smart for my first visit to Regina's place to be work-related? I guess a first visit for work is better than no visit at all. Hell, I met her through work. When we kissed the other day, it was so spontaneous; she's looking for spontaneity and not some pre-planned course of action.

At 8:45am the sun's summer heat has yet to take grip of Georgetown's homogenous asphalt streets and bricked sidewalks. I'm rocking a golf shirt, khaki pants, and loafers. Walking down Reservoir, I first see Regina sitting on the front porch of her townhouse condo.

"Wylie," she shouts, waving, smiling largely before allowing a certain degree of grimness to consume her demeanor.

"Morning Regina," I say with a one-and-off wave back.

"Come on," she says, waving me towards her impatiently. As I approach closer, her smell and jitters make it quite apparent she's already been in to the coffee this morning. I follow her up a set of carpeted steps through a locked door and in to a small living room. On her coffee table and sofa, opened books and scribbled-on legal pads lie everywhere. She clears a place for us on the couch and sits me down next to her.

"I can tell you're excited. What is it?"

"First off," she says. "If I tell you something, if I share a theory of mine with you, then will you promise me you won't think I'm schizo?"

"Without a doubt. Shoot," I say.

"Look at this," she says. She thrusts a book authored by a familiar person in to my hands: Professor Kimball Catchello.

"I'm actually familiar with both the book and its author. What's your take?" I ask.

"Look at the evidence cited by the latest works of these six authors. All the books were published contemporaneously, within a span of four months from oldest to latest publication. Usually it takes a year for a book to traverse the publication process, yet each of these books cite the other as evidence. I've dug in to all institutional reports cited in these books; these professors are intimately related to all their sources of "new" evidence by one direct connection or another. In most circumstances, their claims are verified via circular references. Here, look at this rough chart I've drawn up. It's a prime example." I examine a simple diagram. At the top is scribbled Catchello's name, and arrows link his name to chillingly familiar names below: Silviano, Chandler, Lockington and Kasowski.

"They manipulate, distort, or entirely omit established historical facts and scientific precepts while relying on facts whose significance is disproportionately distorted, down to even citing new facts that each of these writers credit to another of their fellows, and they obscure the origin and merits of these facts in doing so. These books, when viewed collectively, indicate a *conspiracy* to subvert some of the foundational precepts of academic integrity. In other words, they're abusing their positions and relative authority in the field to campaign for their own capricious beliefs," Regina says.

"Geez," I say as I listen to the methodology and conclusion of Regina's investigation while reading over her notes.

"How did you put all this together?"

"Just staying abreast of the latest work in my field. The conclusions the researchers were arriving at were so diametrically-opposed to standard interpretation, even politically charged, that I couldn't help but dig deeper in to their evidence and methodology," she says.

"My God, you're incredible. It takes a real mind to uncover something like this from scratch," I say.

Regina blushes. "But I don't know what to do about this academic treason. School didn't exactly teach me what to do in this situation. Besides, tattle-tales aren't thought of as the coolest kids on the playground," she says.

"You're not alone," I say as I clinch her hand. "And in this case, I think revealing the truth is the right thing to do. On an important aside, I have some things to tell you. The conclusions of my investigation, I arrived at them following different methods, but they're alarmingly convergent with your theory. I met with Raul

140

Aquino. He tells me that this group, the American Historical Association, used to be a large democratic body of historians. So long ago; however, all but a handful of the elite historians were turned out of the group. Currently, it's ruled by this oligarchy."

"We have to do something," Regina declares angrily, jumping to her feet and pacing once across the room to the open window overlooking the campus of Georgetown University.

"It may be a long shot, but I think I know what we should do next. I'm the first to admit it's somewhat self-interested, but if we find it I think it solves all our problems."

"What's the panacea?" she asks.

"Finkel's last book. I believe it exists. I believe he kept it secret *even from you* because it was going to out the corruption of the AHA and dispel all credibility from their fabricated neo-history. I believe they either stole it moments after he died *or perhaps he was even killed for it*." Regina hobbles back over to the couch and collapses beside me. Her skin assumes a pale white hue. It's apparent my revelation has caused her some psychological stress.

"You really think they would have *killed* him? Over a historical interpretation?"

"I think it's within the realm of plausibility that they killed him to silence his authoritative interpretation of history, which at the moment has broad-ranging political implications. Regina last night, I was supposed to meet Professor Silviano for drinks. Only when I met him, he wasn't alone. He was having drinks with Congressman Callahan who's one of the co-sponsors of the legislation to expand the 13th Amendment. They need a formidable team of intellectuals to attack the Christians and other groups who support the prevailing moral code to back off, so they'll have enough space to re-write the law to satisfy their own whim and desire. In the process, a few

141

groups win at the expense of society: the atheist conspirators dethrone God as the greatest intellect in the Universe and thus ascend to the throne themselves; the politicians behind the movement to expand the 13th amendment want to consolidate their power by giving the masses what they want—a thinly veiled form of communism; the bottom-half of society gets a leg up in economic terms. The problem, of course, is that they'll unhinge the fundamental working parts of the greatest machine of human wealth creation ever brought to fruition. At first, this will all seem great because it will seem our politicians finally found the gumption to annihilate the social ills of the unequal distribution of wealth. Good times will pursue, perhaps even for as long as a decade or two. But an insidious, festering problem will begin to decay the pillars of civilization, and because of all the jubilant glee it will go unnoticed: the amount of wealth produced by American industry will drop precipitously. Sooner or later, we'll exhaust our stored wealth and the effect of the expansion of the 13th amendment will reverse our society from one of progress to one of hyper-regression. And all for the best of intentions," I say.

"That's some heavy shit dude. In all seriousness, do you honestly believe someone would kill Professor Finkel due to belief in some abstract future state of events such as you just described?" she asks.

"That really just depends, doesn't it? Even if it is all completely true, none of it matters unless we can prove it. If we can find Al's missing manuscript, then we could *at least* make a circumstantial case for foul play," I say.

"Ok, but let's say Al really did write this manuscript and kept it secret from almost everyone. Then let's assume either the AHA or some affiliate of theirs killed Al to suppress his authoritative knowledge. Then why wouldn't they destroy every last shred of evidence, including the manuscript they're trying to suppress?"

"That's a great question. A totally rational criminal would go to great pains to destroy all the links between his or herself and their crime. Thankfully, people and especially criminals are rarely if ever entirely rational. Some criminals take something from the scene of the crime as a 'token' of their 'achievement.' Also, maybe there were sections of the book that another author could appropriate to further his own work. In sum, even though it was very detrimental to their cause, it would still possess a great intrinsic value. Certainly, the publishers advanced enough money in the hopes of having the book written," I say.

"If someone were likely to have it, then who would have it?" Regina asks.

"As far as I can tell, Silviano and Callahan are at the top of this thing. If you could get to him, Callahan seems drunk enough to talk again. But as far as someone who would have kept a copy of the manuscript, my money's on Silviano. He's academic and all those guys collect books. Perhaps even keeping the book would be Silviano's great insult to Finkel, concealing his nemesis's magnum opus from the sight of the world."

"Neither of them know me. I could try to get close to them," she says.

"No. I'd worry for your safety."

"But I worry for *everyone's* safety if I don't do it," she says.

I know she's right. I take her hand and hold it in my own and smile in to her eyes encouragingly. Soon after this, we both quietly brainstorm our strategy. Regina is furiously scribbling notes and conducting research on her i-Pad. I, on the other hand, stare lethargically at her rotating ceiling fan. I can't tell whether her fan blades really are or are just made to look like woven-grass fans. I finally decide that it really doesn't matter.

"Ok, I've got it," Regina says. "I'm going to play the basics. I'll discover which coffee shop or restaurant Silviano frequents, dress like a slutty coed and conspicuously read Nietzsche and have a pile of similar books next to me. I'll strike up a conversation with him and find a way to have myself invited over to his house. About the time I arrive, you can provide a brief distraction that will give me just enough time to download his computer's hard drive and give a cursory glance to his bookshelves. I realize it leaves a lot of room for error, but it feels really exciting," she says. "Hello, Wylie are you listening to me?"

I suddenly realize I've been staring blankly at the ceiling, gently rubbing an ink pen across the top of my lower set of teeth. "It's definitely a start," I finally manage to say. I feel a pit of worry welling up in my belly for Regina. The last thing I want to do is let Regina get hurt, or even let down if we don't turn up anything. Still, even if it doesn't work out we can always publicize our own findings accusing the AHA of impropriety, perhaps under this movement to expand the 13th Amendment and at least finish Al's work, even if we aren't able to seek justice for his death. Then there is also the issue of my employers' displaced interest.

Eventually we both agree to reconvene at Regina's condo tomorrow morning. I'll stalk Silviano, and once he settles in someplace public, Regina will move in to make contact with him. I've also enlisted Carter to help out. If Regina is successful getting inside Silviano's house, then I'll dispatch Carter disguised as Fed Ex to draw Silviano's attention away from Regina long enough to allow her to download his hard drive and skim through his library.

It's a shot in the dark, but hopefully we'll at least know more tomorrow afternoon than we know today.

Back at my apartment, I flip on the TV to breaking news. A newsman is live on the lawn of Capitol Hill.

"This is Bob Weinghart for Capitol Political News with a breaking story. Much to the chagrin of the odds makers, legislation to expand the 13th Amendment, the so-called 'Affluence for All' law, has just passed the Senate by a vote of 78-21. Now unlike regular legislation, which would normally go to the President, this bill will actually go to the states to be voted on either by their legislatures or ratifying conventions. From there, it will require 38 states to assent before the Archivist of the United States certifies the amendment, officially making it law," Weinghart says. Throngs of disorganized demonstrations yell out of unison, and carry mismatched signs in the periphery. "With me now is noted political scientist Graham Greenbag of Galt University. Dr. Greenbag, given your prowess for political clairvoyance, how do you see the states receiving this suggestion from their Congress to amend the United States Constitution?"

"Thanks for having me on Bob. You know, Americans take their Constitution pretty seriously, which is in contrast to a lot of other countries. Take Mexico for example. Pretty much every act of their national legislature *is* a constitutional amendment. It's pretty different here where we haven't had a constitutional amendment ratified since 1992. Still, you know, there is a lot of popular support for this bill," Dr. Greenbag says. A map of the United States is now shown concurrently beside the two talking heads. "You know, this is going to be an ironic vote. A lot of the country's greatest centers of wealth reside in traditionally blue states. This bill was originally proposed by the Democrats, but what you're going to see happen is

145

that some of these traditionally wealthy blue states are going to fall somewhere between close calls or likely-to-vote against the measure. This may seem confounding at first, but it actually makes a lot of logical sense. Those who stand to lose vested interests will fight against the measure, in such places as New York and Massachusetts. On the other hand, places that stand to gain, such as most of the South, are likely to vote *for* the bill. It really is an interesting, paradigm-shifting dynamic," Dr. Greenbag says.

"Great, great program. Dr. Greenbag only seconds before the station airs the next program. Do you have a prediction for us today?"

"Given the current momentum of this social movement, coupled with herd behavior and information cascades, the widespread support for Affluence for All from many sectors of the economy, ethnicities, and other major groups—*I say it passes with forty-four states assenting. . .*"

I cut off the TV. I've got my work cut out for me. It's difficult work, being caught on the wrong side of history.

Chapter 15

Good heavens are the words on my lips when I first see Regina on the day of our coup. She's wearing a white sleeveless button-down shirt knotted above the waist, exposing her well-conditioned abdomen. Her daisy duke jean shorts are cut short, above the pocket. She has her hair done in pigtails. She's also decided to wear her thick-rimmed glasses, a tantalizing maneuver.

"I like your disguise," she says when she spots me coming up the sidewalk. I'm wearing a flaming pink tank top with the letters: RUN BKK. I've got an Obey Propaganda hat pulled over my bushy hair and sunglasses wrapped around my eyes to further conceal my identity.

"I like yours better," I hear myself saying. Regina smiles big, as if not so much at my comment as at me, or so I like to think anyway. Together we walk along Reservoir towards the Wisconsin bus stop. For this time of morning, the Circulator is surprisingly empty.

"There must be a bus or two just in front of this one," Regina observes. I nod in agreement. I feel a canyon of nervousness crater in my belly, but I keep my feelings to myself. After all, Regina is the one really being called on to perform today, and she doesn't need her mood afflicted by my skittishness. Looking her over, Regina appears cool and ready. Besides, her intrinsic beauty is enough to distract even the strongest of intellects. Now I unfortunately become cognizant of the origin of my anxiety. Of course I'm not worried about my physical safety, I'm worried about Regina's safety and the psychological harm it would cause me if something were to happen to her. To be rational, my fears don't necessarily reflect the intentions of Silviano to any degree of accuracy. After all, he doesn't even know what's about to happen: we're going to pull one of the oldest and most successful cons on him in the book: (1) stalk, (2) seduce, (3) divert attention, (4) conduct reconnaissance, (5) exit. The plan is that simple.

After we arrive at GW, I leave Regina posted up at a local coffee shop and I start skateboarding around outside of Silviano's office building. Carter texts me that he's in position in a non-descript rental van in a Fed Ex costume. Everything is in place. It's 10:15am. No sign of Silviano as of yet.

I shred a loop between Farragut Metro Station and the World Bank headquarters. I thrash pass grey and black suits, security guards, capitol police, hipsters, preppy students, homeless, tourists from all over America, tourists from all over the World, people in this profession and that profession, sights and smells of international cuisine restaurants, anxious cars honk their horns and speed through the major intersection at the sight of green light. Skating, I carefully scan the sidewalk for rocks and other debris, which could potentially send me tumbling to a scathing injury. A group of three younger skateboarders pass by and shoot me dirty looks. A police officer watches me hawkishly, as if I may be infected by some peculiarly powerful strain of anarchy that requires immediate attention, lest I cause a tear in the fabric of the law-and-order continuum with the potential to cause cement to dematerialize and return civilization's great achievements back in to the ash from which it came.

Group text from Regina to Carter and I: "Status?"

"Still nothing," I respond.

I skateboard and skateboard. My legs start to grow weary. I take a seat on a bench facing the main entrance to Silviano's office building. I glimpse at my phone. It's 12:36 pm and still no sign of

Silviano. I just hope he came in to the office this morning before we set up the stake out. I'm getting a lot of sun in this skimpy outfit. I should have put on some sun block. The least I could do for myself is move to the shade. Across the way is a dry looking spot under a shade tree. I pick up my skateboard and start to head over when I feel someone's presence hovering behind me. I turn and see the police officer who was watching me earlier.

"You a student here?" he asks. I quickly discern that he's a - University cop by reading the insignia on his badge.

"Nah, just a sojourner brah. Taking a rest brah," I say. He makes it immediately apparent that I've insulted him in some form or manner. Maybe it's because I didn't use my humbled-citizen voice.

"If you aren't a student, then it would be *wise* for you to be moving along," he says. He thumbs around on his belt and rests his palm on what I recognize to be a telescopic baton, or what is basically a child's light saber toy only made out of aluminum instead of plastic—a formidable blunt force weapon.

"Yeah brah. The boarding ain't much around here brah," I say. I stand and start to leave when I catch a glimpse of Silviano exiting the office building. Unfortunately, he's also keenly observing my exchange with the police officer, but given my disguise and distance, I'm able to avoid recognition.

"Late brah," I say and move at an angle towards the tail of Silviano's current trajectory. "Got him," I text Regina and Carter. I follow him around two corners and watch him disappear through a set of doors. "He's in Café Lombardy."

"I'm moving," Regina says. While I'm still staking the place out, Regina passes me on her way to meet her mark. "Wish me luck," she whispers. Just as I begin to open my mouth she leans in and kisses me on the cheek. My face begins to tingle. Before I'm able to do anything else, she's opening the door and walking in to the café. I feel this admixture of emotions working on me once again, confusing my intentions. It's difficult watching a girl you like walk in to a café to use her looks to deceive and manipulate another man. It's a situation I've never contemplated finding myself in.

I get anxious from standing on the sidewalk with neither visibility nor insight as to what's going on inside that café. I decide to do a skate-by and take a peek in. As I peer in, I see our plan is already working. Silviano and Regina are sitting at a table talking around her stack of Dawkins, Nietzsche, and Foucault books. She even has that son of a bitch smiling a lurid, grotesque smile. I pick a new post as far away from the entrance as possible while still within visibility. Now it's time for Regina to answer the big if: Can she coax Silviano in to leaving with her?

"What's going on?" Carter group texts.

"I don't know. I don't have a vantage point," I reply. No response from Regina.

"You know these vans are pretty cozy. Taking a nap in one of the back seats with the AC on—money," Carter texts.

"You'd better not fall asleep," I text.

"Don't fall asleep? Then what the hell is there a ringer on my phone for?" Carter texts.

"Just don't. I'm under enough stress," I text.

"Silviano is paying his bill," Regina texts. "U 2 relax. I'm following him to his house to borrow a book now."

Oh shit. "Taxi!" I successfully hail the first cab to pass. "Take me to the cross street between 13th and 14th street off of Corcoran Street in Dupont," I instruct the driver. Soon we're racing off.

"Just let me out at this white van," I tell the cabbie. I flip him a twenty and smack the glass on the van. Carter is in there asleep with his hat pulled down over his face to shield his eyes from the blazing sun.

"Carter!" I yell and smack the window violently until he rouses. "Carter! Wake the fuck up!"

Text from Regina: "In a blue taxi."

"Fuck." I yell as Carter finally sits up, his hat falling to his lap as he opens his eyes, much to my relief. He unlocks the van and I fling the door open. "You're stressing me out."

"Just chill out dude. After all, I took off work to do you this favor," Carter says.

"Well the favor doesn't do anyone any good if the whole thing gets blotched right in the critical moment."

"Nothing's blotched. Look I'm alert and ready to do my job. Now if *you* don't want to blotch the thing you'd better make yourself scarce," Carter says. And he's right. I run across the street and dip in to a little coffee shop called "Le Diplomate." I can't help but to stare down at my illuminated phone screen, eagerly waiting to see how this thing will unfold.

"What can I get you?" a waitress asks, interrupting my compulsive staring.

"House coffee and a ham and cheese baguette please," I say, giving only an instant's worth of eye contact to the server.

"Would you like me to bring a condiment tray?"

"Yes. The works."

"They're here," Carter texts. "I'm in position." "They're going inside. I'm waiting for the signal."

Regina is supposed to send a single-symbol text to cue Carter. More than ever, the suspense is wearing on my nerves. So close to the decisive moment. I begin to perceive the autonomic physiological processes of my internal organs and it gives me immense anxiety. The waiter places my coffee and baguette before me, and he says something. Only I can't hear. I glance at him briefly again before returning to my single-minded fixation to my phone screen. My heart begins to palpitate irrhymatically. Then my phone vibrates and I shiver.

"!" Regina texts. My heart beat transforms in to a loud and steady thud. I can feel my heart eating in every remote crevice of my body. Even the tips of my toes are pulsating.

"Moving," Carter texts. I quickly move over to the window, but it's a bad angle and I can't see anything. Each second feels like an hour. I feel so helpless, so impotent even. I just want to tear out of this café and assist, but I know if I do I'll spoil the whole thing. Two minutes elapse. The more time to pass between communication the better. Three minutes elapse. Four minutes elapse. I'm looking out the window and see Carter's van, but that's it. Then I see Carter return to the van, start the ignition, and drive away. But what's happened to Regina?

"Status?" I text. No response after a minute. "Update? What's going on?" Sitting inactive in this café is like standing by while acid burns through my skin. I feel all the pain of losing Regina, and it reawakens the pain of losing Angie. I feel depressed. I feel my prefrontal cortex shutting down as my limbic system begins to take control. My once razor-sharp thoughts start to become cloudy and mushy. I want to panic, even if in public, if for nothing more than to reaffirm to myself that I'm still alive.

Carter texts me. "You're not going to believe who showed and walked in while I was distracting Silviano."

"Who?"

152

"Penelope."

"Penelope who?"

"Penelope the girls we went out with a couple of times recently?"

"Why the hell is Penelope at Silviano's?" I text before placing a phone call to Carter.

"Wile."

"Where are you now?"

"I just pulled around the block. Where are you?"

"I'm at Le Diplomate a block away," I say. I try to angle myself to see Silviano's front porch, but to no avail. I open the front door and ease down the sidewalk along Silviano's street, but I'm careful to keep a safe distance. "Why the hell would Penelope know Silviano? What the odds—wait."

"What?" Carter asks.

"Get here quick," I say. Silviano and Penelope are dragging Regina out to a Cadillac. Regina's wrists are bound. I watch in horror as I sprint towards them and watch Penelope strike Regina in the face.

"Stop!" I yell out. Silviano hears me and turns for an instant. The sly smile sends shivers down my spine as I burst in to a full-on sprint. "Carter get here now. They're kidnapping Regina!"

"Goddamit I'm trapped on a one-way street," Carter yells.

"They're getting away," I scream as the car speeds away. I run for as long as I can, but my legs are no match for the sedan's speed. Three blocks up they take a left turn and disappear from sight. Five minutes later Carter returns to the block.

"Hop in Wile, let's go."

"She's gone," I cry, tears pouring from my eyes. "They got her and they're gone."

Carter hops out of his van and wraps his arms around me. "Shh it's alright little brother. We'll get her back. We'll get her back." In my moment of deepest despair, I spot a shard of hope lying on the ground. The glimmer from a metallic object has caught my eye, and I break free from Carter's embrace to rush over to it. It's Regina's purse!

"Carter look," I say, holding it up. I unzip the purse to find nothing other than an external hard drive!

"Pretty little devil accomplished her objective, she just got pinched in the process. Look Wile, I know you're upset but this hard drive might have the answer to all our problems. If we can implicate Silviano, then he'll probably deliver Regina for a plea deal."

"Let's hope," I say. "But for now, time is of the essence." I end my call to Carter which has been ongoing, and dial 911.

Shortly after Regina's kidnapping, Carter and I are at the nearest police precinct filing a police report. We're waiting in a detective's office when the officer with whom we filed the report and another enter the room.

"I'm Detective Bill Gavern, and this is my partner Lee Dinsmore. We understand you're concern for your lady friend, but as far as investigating a Doctor Anthony Silviano, well, there's been a restraining order filed against you. I don't suppose you've received notification of this."

"What do you mean a restraining order?"

"It appears several history professors around town are grumbling that you've been stalking and harassing them. Two of them have filed a complaint, and four others have filed affidavit's in support of the complaints. It appears as though based on the prestige

154

of the complainants the restraining order will likely issue,"
Detective Gavern says.

"This is bullshit!" I yell, jumping to my feet with my heart racing a thousands beats a minute.

"Woah, now hold on just a minute," Detective Dinsmore says. "I've done some inquiring and it turns out you're girlfriend is out of town visiting her sister. I was just on the phone with Cris Damasio and she says her sister called her from the airport just before we spoke on the phone. Regina is heading to Chicago. Now we see you're upset and I'll be glad to check back in with the girls after Regina's flight has landed."

"I saw her get kidnapped."

"Did you see the girl get kidnapped?" Dinsmore asks Carter.

"Well, no, but we were with her! We were, um. . ."

"Stalking Silviano," Gavern says.

"Nah, that's not we were doing. We were investigating."

"Do you have a private investigators license?" Gavern asks Carter.

"Well, no. But I was operating on Wylie's."

"That's not how the system works. You've technically committed a Class 2 misdemeanor, punishable by 6 months jail time and up to a $5,000 fine."

"Oh," Carter replies.

"Oh is right," Gavern says. "Now listen Mr. Wainwright. I'm sorry your girlfriend has left town without telling you, but her leaving town *is not* pretext for you to be stalking and harassing reputable citizens of the District. Now you've basically confessed to stalking Doctor Silviano. I know times can be hard when you're unemployed, I've got a kid brother who's been out of work for six months, and I know it can cause a lot of psychological distress especially when you're having lady troubles. But you can't just manufacture reasons to go—"

"I'm not unemployed goddamit. I'm a licensed private investigator with a contract to investigate the loss of a missing manuscript. I have every reason to believe that Anthony Silviano ordered the death of Professor Al Finkel to succeed him as the greatest living historian and to distort the course of future political events. I'm not a lunatic! This shit is real."

"That's enough Mr. Wainwright. Now, I'm gathering that you're a deeply troubled young man. I recommend you get some psychological counseling. Now I'm going to ask you to leave my office and drop this whole matter, leave Silviano and his colleagues alone, and wait on your girlfriend to call you *or* we'll be compelled to find you in contempt of the restraining order that's being issued against you. I'm a compassionate man, Mr. Wainwright, but everyone has their limits," Gavern says.

"Come on, let's go Wylie," Carter says, wrapping his arms around me and escorting me from the police station. I shake myself loose from his grasp once we're outside. The pulsating, rhythmless traffic only aggravates my frustration.

"*Fuck!*" I yell to the top of my lungs until I feel blood vessels bulging in my neck and face. "It's all my fault," I lament, switching immediately from anger to despair. "It's all my fault. I put her up to this, now who *knows* what they'll do to her."

"You gotta calm down Wile. Listen, I know some guys over in the Southeast who may be able to help us. I hate to use them, but they've got a certain specialty in extra-legal judicial process. I'm gonna take you home, and I'll roll over and talk to them about providing us with their services. You get to work on researching the external hard drive and see if you can't find anything to pin on

156

Silviano. The police will give us their attention if you can find a smoking gun on him. If you can't find it, then maybe my friends can help."

"I guess you're way is the only thing left to do."

"It most certainly is. Now come on, let me drive you home," Carter says.

Back at my place, I don't waste much time firing up my computer and accessing Silviano's hard drive to see what it has in store for me. While his hard drive is uploading, I give the web a cursory search. *Fuck*, I think to my self when I see that *10* states are set to vote on the AFA tomorrow, and analysts anticipate all 10 will vote to ratify the measure. To further exacerbate my feelings of hopelessness, once Silviano's hard drive has synced with my computer, it informs me its contents are password protected. I try a couple of obvious passwords, but surrender for the moment in frustration. I click "forgot password." The security question is "He invented the bubble." No one invented the bubble, I surmise, this must be a riddle only Silviano knows the answer to. It would take either an expert computer hacker or cryptologist to unlock this thing.

Frustrated at my own lack of leads, I text Carter to check the status on his end.

"Status?"

"I was just texting you Wylie. I got in touch with my boys. We've got a meeting with them tomorrow in the AM. I'll text you later to firm up the details.," Carter texts.

I feel so impotent waiting around just to meet other people to beg them to clean up my mess. The scene of Regina being drug in to that car just plays over and over again and again in my head. I feel so guilty. I put her up to this job and then I just stood by and watched her disappear in to the maze of D.C. streets. I keep thinking about empowerment. Then my mind registers my next move: I'm going to get myself a gun.

An hour later I'm at the DMV of all places looking for the "DL Exchange." I find it, down a undistinguished, poorly lit hallway. I'm already baffled by why I've come to a DMV instead of a more familiar sportsman's store, but I figure I've come this far. Three-quarters the way down the hall I read a small, nonchalant sign that reads DL Exchange. I knock on the door.

"You may enter."

I walk through the door. Sitting at the desk is a woman in her mid-to-late thirties. Various papers are shuffled all about her desk. Two bottles of nail polish sit unopened in a small cleared-off area; one of her feet is up on the desk with her pant leg rolled back. She takes a bottle of what I recognize to be nail polish remover, applies a small dab to a cotton swab, and begins scrubbing one of her nails.

"I said you can come in," she reiterates.

"Oh, it's just that I think I'm in the wrong place."

"Which place are you looking for?" she asks without looking up from her task at hand.

"I'm looking for the gun shop, or it's D.C. equivalent."

"You've found it," she says, looking up from her job to give me a once over. "Only I hate to burst your bubble," she says, flicking her short hair out of her face with a jerk of the neck, " but unless you've got a permit, you can't buy a gun today. And it takes about a year for a permit to process."

"A year is about how long I've had my permit," I say.

She puts her feet on the ground, sits up straight, starts placing her nail polish and associated materials in a desk drawer while peppering me with questions.

"You got a permit a year ago and you're just now looking to get a gun?"

"That's right. I'm a private detective, but I never needed a gun before."

"It's hard to get those permits. You must have done something or known someone special."

"I was a lawyer at the FDIC before I picked up this racket."

"Hum, unlikely, but I guess that could explain it. They only issue about 50 of those particular permits a year."

"Really? I knew the number was low, but I wouldn't have guessed it was that low."

"It's supposed to tick up, but who knows? I *like* a lack of business," she says. "It gives me time to work on personal things."

I bet. Like grooming and staring at the fucking wall.

"Look. I need a gun now. Can you help me?"

"I can, but it'll take some time."

"Time for what? You can't just sell me a gun?"

"I don't sell guns. I transfer them. So how it works is you buy a gun somewhere else, but you aren't allowed to bring it in to DC or have it shipped in. It has to come through me. For the service, I charge a small one-time fee of $250."

"That's cheaper than my street parking permit."

"That's a good way of looking at it. I think I'll borrow that observation from you in the future when customers complain about my prices. Shit, it's hard enough to make it as things are."

"I bet," I say. "So you willing to ride over in to Virginia with me?"

"To buy a gun?"

"That's right."

"You really want it today?"

159

"I was hoping to have been walking the street with it five minutes ago. Can you go?"

"Let me ask you this question, Mister?"

"Wylie Wainwright."

"Mister Wainwright, why do you want a gun now after you've had the license a full year? Most people come in and get a gun immediately."

"I never needed one until now."

"What do you need one now for?"

"For protection. Shit hit the fan earlier this morning, and if I'd had a gun the whole thing likely wouldn't have gone down."

"Fair enough."

"What's your name again?

"Donna Loewy, Certified Fire Arm Transfer Agent."

"It's nice to make your acquaintance," I say.

"Like wise."

Donna leans over to roll her pant leg down before rummaging around the office for her belongings. I wouldn't have ever imagined D.C.'s only *legal* arms dealer would be a five-foot five blacked-headed chick.

"You do realize there will be a surcharge for the shop visit."

"No problem."

Crossing the Key Bridge, I can't help but observe that Donna keeps looking down at her three unfinished toe nails: two are painted pink and the other eight are clear. I wonder how self-conscious she is. Oh, there she just buried her toes up under the lower-part of the dashboard. Pretty self-conscious I guess. I hope her self-consciousness doesn't affect the surcharge. Damn, I probably should have gotten her to quote that for me *before* driving her across state lines.

"Which store are we going too?"

"I was heading towards Gander Mountain. Do you know of a better dealer?"

"Of course I do. This is my business. Sid's in Crystal City has the best prices and the best selection. I'll direct you there. Take the second exit."

In a matter of fifteen minutes, I'm walking through the aisles and aisles of guns at Sid's Weapons, Ammunitions and Supply Haus. This place has every conceivable style of pistol, bow and arrow, rifle, shotgun, machine gun, knife, tomahawk, and every other weapon I could imagine.

Once I come to from the overload of options, I look up to see Donna examining a pistol, presumably on her own account. There are so many options that I'm lost in the sea of them. I don't have any particular expertise in picking one gun from another. Just when I begin to think I'll have to lean on either a salesman or Donna to pick, a particular gun catches my eye. A nearby salesman must have seen the spark go off, he is on the scene quickly to assist me.

"See something you like sir?"

"Yes, I'd like to see that silver one there. What do you call that?"

"That's a Smith and Wesson thirty-eight special," the salesman says as he unlocks the case and puts the gun in my hands. "It's light weight, reliable, and is one of the most popular calibers from one of the most popular brands of all time."

"That sounds pretty good," I say. I open up what I guess you call the chamber and spin it around. "What are its pros and cons?"

"Well, besides what I just told you? It's lightweight and concealable. It's also very reliable. This pistol will never jam on you. On the negative side, compared to other guns, it isn't as accurate at longer distances as some pistols and it doesn't hold as many shells. It's a great intimidation device. What are you planning to use it for?"

"I'm a private detective across the Potomac."

"Oh, then this gun is classic for your profession. Especially in D.C. where no one has a gun anyway, you wouldn't really want a 9mm or its equivalent, what, blasting off 15 rounds in to a high population density area. No, this is the piece you want."

"I'll take it."

"Great. If you could just provide me with two forms of ID, I'll get your background check initiated."

"Thanks," I say as I hand him my driver's license and private investigator's license.

Having taken care of my business, I walk over to Donna who is holding what looks like a bazooka. "Finding anything you like?" I ask.

She turns and points the massive rifle at me. I jump out of the way. "Woah, watch where you point that thing."

"Relax. It's unloaded."

"How can you tell?"

"They always keep them unloaded in these stores."

"I'd still rather you not point it at me."

"Fine," she says. "Did you have any luck finding anything? Do you need my help picking something out?"

"No I picked one."

"Yea? What'd you get?"

"Thirty-eight special."

"That's not a good gun."

"Why not?"

"Because they make a lot better guns today. Guns with better accuracy and more bullets. You should get a Glock or a Springfield Armory."

"I'm happy with what I got."

"Ok, well as long as you're happy. Listen, I'm just toying around. After you've paid for the thing, just give it to me so we can get out of here."

"Fine."

After I've paid for the thing, I hand it over to Donna so she can be the one to technically transport it across the Potomac in to D.C. Regulations are so stupid. I bet ten-thousand illicit guns go back and forth across the Potomac everyday unnoticed, but I've got to pay Donna Loewy X-amount to bring mine in to the city. Our drive back in to the city is a quiet one, although traffic is severely congested for the most part. Once we're back in her office, she has me fill out about 15 pages of forms before she prints me off a bill for $450. I tell her I don't have that kind of cash on me, but she says its fine, if I just want to give her my address she can invoice it to me. I thank her for her assistance.

"Be careful how you use that thing," she says as I'm on my way out the door. "They can get you in a lot of trouble."

"Thanks for the tip," I reply.

Chapter 16

I hardly slept last night, tossing and turning in my covers
when I was able to lie down, having nightmares about Regina's
poor treatment, at worst imagining her even dead. At 4am, I resolve
that sleeplessness is better than succumbing to the torture of my
continuing nightmares. Sitting straight up in my bed, I rub my
fingers through my hair incessantly, as though the repetitive practice
will in some way calm me. While I'm stroking my hair and absently
surveying my room, I catch a glimpse of the pistol sitting on my
nightstand. I hop out of bed and clutch it in my hand. The little
portable cannon feels good in my hand. When you think about what
it really is, it's a little device that strikes people dead, at least when
used correctly. That must have frightened the hell out the Indians
when they first encountered them. Rifles looking so much like mere
sticks; white men just striking people dead with them along with
the accompanying roar of the gun powder: the theatre of shooting a
gun is almost as tremendous as its inherent power. Well now I've
got a new trump card against these thugs, but acquired one hand too
late. I deeply regret having not gotten one of these when I first
started this gig, especially considering the danger I knew was
inherent in the occupation. Of course, I was never concerned about
my *own* safety. In fact, I was anti-gun until just yesterday.
Yesterday's events made it explicitly apparent how guns are useful:
they are capable of assisting in the protection of people you care
about. Lesson hard learned. I've got my hopes up that Carter's
connections are as good as he's hyping them up to be.

Looking at myself in the mirror, I start raising the gun to eye level and pointing it at my reflection. Damn, this is a sexy look. Live by the gun, die by the gun. I pull on a pair of jeans, and practice drawing the pistol out of my rear hip pocket. I'm pretty quick at it, actually. There's a notable fluidity in my drawing style, as if my limbs are exactly the right proportion to be a good quick draw. I wonder how accurately I'll shoot the thing? No time to practice now, but at close range I don't suppose it matters.

I occupy my mind as such until Carter calls me at 6am to say he's on the way. I freshen up a little bit, put on some clean clothes, load the pistol, stick it in my waste band and drop an extra five rounds in to my front pants pocket. After receiving a message from Carter that he's arrived, I look at myself in the mirror one last time and breathe. I ask myself a singular question: Would you kill someone today? To save Regina, the answer is yes. I would kill them all.

I don't often venture over in to Southeast D.C., other than to catch an occasional Nats game. There's not a lot of cross-pollination between Georgetown and the Southeast, really. Don't get me wrong, I wish there were, but facts, as well as prejudices, can be a stubborn thing.

"You get any sleep last night Wile? You don't usually got them bags under your eyes."

"No, not really Carter. But I did manage to acquire *this* yesterday," I say before removing the pistol from my waist band.

"Woah, what the hell are you doing with that thing? Trying to shoot your pecker off? Listen, there's a reason I'm taking you to see these boys and it's because they do the indictable work while we sit on the sidelines. You hear?

"So you expect me to play no role? To just give up?"

"Not really. But if this doesn't go exactly as planned Regina might end up worse off and you may end up in jail if you don't end up dead. This Penelope bitch seems like a real hitman. I don't think just owning a gun automatically makes you a badass. I think there's really few badasses in the world. You know they train people in the military to be desensitized to killing. Do you think you're desensitized enough to kill? Because you'll in all likelihood have a split second to decide whether or not to pull that trigger, and if you don't one'll eventually get pulled on you. Listen, I'm in this thing with you. I've got this connection from the old neighborhood. These aren't the fellas I particularly care to call, but they do have some expertise in these, um, blood sport situations."

"Ok, I'll keep this thing put away *unless* there's an emergency."

"Aight. Glad we're on the same page."

We arrive outside of an average seeming auto mechanics garage. A sign out front reads: Riverside Wreckers: Automotive Repair, Repos, On-call towing. Spray painted on a nearby retaining wall are the words: *neighborhood stabilizers*.

"You sure these guys are the ones to handle a kidnapping?" I ask.

"Positive. They advertise their vanilla security business as a side gig, but I know these guys been in the black market strong-arm and surveillance market for as long ask I've been around. I'd reckon the garage is profitable, but it's also sort of a cover. Dig?"

"Yea, I dig. We just can't mess this thing up man. I can't let anything happen to Regina or I would never let myself live it down."

Just as I'm finishing my sentence, I notice this huge black dude, probably 6'5 dressed in black jeans and a black short-sleeve button down shirt with his tank top and gold chain exposed and curly black chest hairs hanging out, beginning to approach us.

"Watch ya'll want?" he asks.

"What's up Steve? It's Carter Ellis. I know you from back when I was a—"

"When you was a grasshopper. I see those private schools your parents sent you off to are keeping you in fine clothes and wheels. Alright. Now why you rolling up to my place?"

"I talked to Pete last night. We've got some business with you guys today."

"Mahn, I ain't go no business wit you. Why don't you go on and get out of here."

"We need you're help," I interject.

"Talking to me crack? I crack dat head open," Steve says.

I see anger flash across Carter's face. Another guy comes running up from inside the garage now, a skinny guy in long black jean shorts hanging below his ass and just wearing a white tank top over his chest.

"Cool it Pete," the guy says. "These are the guys we're meeting with today."

"That's Punchy Pete, guy I talked to," Carter says while the two other guys are talking amongst themselves. The bigger one, Steve, turns back to us.

"My bad fellas. I thought we was runnin' a different score today. You know, years in the business and I still get stressed on game day." Steve says.

"Yea, we're good fellas. We're just waiting on the rest of our boys in the garage to finishing packing up," Pete says, before

167

shooting an erstwhile glance over each shoulder, before leaning in closer over the vehicle passenger window. "Listen, we found the trick yall looking for. Penelope Lee. They got another name for her on the street though. Out here they call her the Blight. She's rumored to have carried out at least 5 or so hits since she came on the scene. She's no freelancer either. Word has it she's plugged in to some organization, maybe even connected with some power around the city."

"So what's the move?" Carter asks.

"You know, we don't usually touch things that cross the power. But you saved our license several years back, and we haven't forgotten that. Today, we're just going to pull a standard bait and pinch. You two are riding along, but just as spectators. You understand me?"

Carter and I both sit there in rapt attention.

"That was a question boys."

"I understand you," I say.

"Yea," Carter says.

"Aight listen. I got all my boys rolling with. We got this all planned out. Ya'll don't need to know nothing else till it's done. Park your car over there and load up with me. We're rolling in ten."

Carter and I get in a Tahoe SUV with deeply tinted windows with Pete, Steve and one other dude. We follow a tow truck with two other dudes in it. Sitting at every streetlight seems like an eternity. A million possible scenarios stream through my imagination and all of them are anxiety laden. It's like I can't even imagine seeing Regina again. My palms are clammy. I continue to catch myself rocking my leg anxiously. I deliberately try to control all of these outward manifestations of my anxiety, but it's difficult considering how genuinely nervous I am. The cold steel of the pistol

168

presses against my belly. My thoughts flash back to my quick draw practice early this morning. The extra bullets press firmly against my thigh through my pocket. This moment is all too real. I feel the regret of having not been better prepared for this moment, of having to trust absolute strangers to resolve the situation, of quitting detective work entirely after this case so that no one is ever again hurt by my lack of experience. But not long after we've entered the familiar streets of Adams Morgan, passing all of the International restaurants, bars, head shop, pedestrians, old apartment buildings, we turn down a residential street and then another before parking at the entry to a street that terminates at a dead end.

"Set to work," Steve says into a CB radio.

"Aight," is the response.

The tow truck pulls up to a car, *the car* I saw Regina kidnapped in.

"Wait here," Steve says. Steve and his operative cock their pistols, hop out of the SUV, and stealthily run around the back of the house. Meanwhile, the two tow truck guys get out and each circle Penelope's car once, before one of them hops back in the truck and backs it up to the car. They're making a lot noise, between hollering at one another and the natural noise of the tow truck.

"It's not working," I mumble before exclaiming in the shakiest voice, "it's not working!"

"Easy lover. The boys know what they doing," Pete says.

I start to open the car door when Pete grabs me by the shoulder. "Let the boys handle this. She'll make you in an instant and hightail it out of here or finish your girl. If your girl is in that house, my boys ul'll find her. Theys experts at finding hidden girls, drugs, money, you name it."

The sedan is connected to the tow truck now being raised up on to the flat bed. Just like Steve had said, the front door opens and out comes Penelope screaming and waving her arms.

"Hey, you don't have to do that," she yells.

The tow truck guys don't look up.

"Hey," I hear her yell again.

She walks right up to the one on the ground and taps him on the shoulder. He turns to face her and she leans in to make herself heard when he suddenly wraps her up with his arms and falls to the ground on top of her.

"Sit tight," Pete commands as he jumps out of the car and hurries over to assist.

"Goddamn good show," Carter says enthusiastically. He looks over at me to see I don't approve of his spectator mentally. "Sorry Wile. I mean, going to plan."

In just a moment, Steve and his operative carry Penelope quickly over to our SUV and throw her in the trunk. Carter and I turn to look at the bitch, who is bound at the wrists and ankles.

"I bet you *thought* you were one clever bitch," Carter says.

"Fuck you."

"Where is Regina?" I demand.

Penelope spits in my face. I withdraw the pistol from my waistband, pull back the hammer and press the nuzzle against Penelope's forehead. "WHERE IS REGINA?"

"You don't have the balls."

"I orchestrated this operation, didn't I?"

Steve climbs back in the car. "Oh shit. Carter."

"Wylie we don't need to kill her," Carter says.

"It's not in the plan, we need her," Pete says. "We need Penelope alive for the plan."

"Fuck the plan. She's either going to tell us where Regina is or she's going to die."

"Wylie look," Carter says, pulling on my shoulder and directing my attention to the front door of the house. Steve and his operative are helping Regina out of the house and directing her towards the SUV.

"She's alive," I say. Then there's a tug on the pistol, which causes me reflexively to pull on the trigger. *Bang.* Everyone jumps to look over the back seat. Apparently, when we all turned our attention for a brief instant to Regina, Penelope had leaned up, placed her lips around the gun, bit on the site and tried to pull it from my hand. The maneuver inadvertently caused me to put a bullet through the back of her skull. Blood is just gushing out the back of her head and oozing out of her mouth.

"Cold blooded," Carter says.

"That will cost extra," Steve says.

Regina starts to resist walking any closer towards the car after the gun shot rings out. Carter notices, rolls down his window, and entreats her to hurry up. Urgency is written across the faces of both Steve and his operative. Regina hops in and jumps in to Carter's arms, before noticing me and sliding over to give me a hug of relief as well.

"You two saved me," she says.

"We were kind of obligated," I say.

"Yea, you were. What's that," Regina says. Everyone tries to stop her, but it's too late. She's looked in the back seat and seen Penelope's corpse. She shrieks, but everyone admonishes her to maintain her composure. Steve climbs back in to the car. He takes a computer bag off his shoulder and passes it to me.

171

"There wasn't much in the house other than that. A table, chairs, two beds. We found your girl here caged in a soundproofed room. Nothing else there. It was bare."

"This computer may be exactly what we need," I say.

"Right on," Steve says.

We drive slowly out of the neighborhood before flooring it through a few other back streets then on to the beltway. Steve unfolds a blanket and lays it over Penelope, I guess to at least cover her from the sight of passing semi-trucks and passenger buses. We continue passed the suburbs and eventually in to Delaware. Eventually we arrive at a junk yard. We wait in a line behind three other trucks, each with a construction company insignia on their doors, waiting in line to dump their scrap. Although the trucks in front of us all turn right and follow signs to the designated dump area, we turn left and pass by several piles of vehicle carcasses, discarded appliances and the like. Eventually we arrive in what may be described as a seven/eighths circular valley of scrap heap piled three stories high. Across the open area is a camouflaged tarp. A shiny SUV idles inside. We pull up driver's side to driver' side.

"Is it messy?" The Asian driver of the other SUV asks.

Pete, who's driving our SUV, shrugs. "Average one-out job," he tells the Asian dude.

"Let's switch vehicles," Steve says. We all unload and switch vehicles with the Asian fellow. Just as I'm about to climb in to the new SUV, Steve grabs me. "Give the scrubber your pistol. He'll make sure it's never seen again."

I'm reluctant to give up my new pistol, especially since it could attach me to the killing of Penelope, especially since I don't know any of these people before today, but they did get us out of a real pinch and I have no real reason not to trust them. I pull the pistol out of waistband and give it to the Asian scrubber. He nods, hops in the SUV, and pulls out of the hidden crevice with a trail of dust behind him.

"It was starting to stink in there," Carter says.

"You thought so?" Steve says. "I guess I'm used to it."

I don't know whether or not he's kidding.

Chapter 17

Back in D.C., we all take the next day off to relax. Regina understandably doesn't feel safe staying at her place, so she crashes at mine. After listening to just music and napping most of the day, we listen to the TV in the evening to learn four additional states have approved the AFA constitutional amendment and another three are voting tomorrow. TV pundits predict the constitutional amendment to pass within the next two weeks. By the time the news segment has concluded, Regina is already opening Penelope's computer to sift through it for clues. I tell her about Silviano's external hard drive she nabbed and about my troubles getting passed the password screen. "Who invented the bubble. We'll have to hire a computer geek or cryptologist, don't you think."

"John Law," Regina says.

"No, I don't think the law is going to help us here. You know, maybe if we tried the police again they could use their resources to try and open it."

"No, the answer to the question is John Law. He created the first *financial* bubble in France in the 18th Century, haphazardly using financial techniques he had learned in the Netherlands. The French were so clueless, they just turned everything over to him, Central Banking, printing paper currency, tax collection, operating their international trade monopoly, creating and operating the stock market. Many French invested everything in John Law's Mississippi Trading Company stock, but it never produced anything because the land just wasn't settled at all. This was all well before New Orleans ever came in to existence. The feedback loop just caused a buying frenzy, but because there were no *real* profits behind it all, because it was all really just one big ponzi scheme, most of that paper wealth just vanished in to thin air and really damaged the French economy for quite some time. They wouldn't again dabble in modern financial innovations for another few generations," Regina says.

John Law, I type as the answer to the security question. To my amazement, the screen asks me to create a new password. Regina was right. But of course she's right, she's a freaking genius.

"Ok, so I guess we spend our time sifting through these files until we find hard evidence?" I ask.

"Time to roll up our sleeves Wylie," Regina says. We both set up our computers and start to work.

"Wylie, come over here." I walk over and sit next to her on the floor with legs crossed under the coffee table. "I'm going through each of his desktop folders one at a time."

"Why not just do a control—f smart search?"

"That would work, only Al never put his name on his manuscripts until they were ready to be sent to the publishers. I smart searched him, along with a couple of other relevant terms, but found nothing. Like I said, this isn't really surprising given my knowledge of his methods," Regina says.

"Sure," I say.

"Unfortunately, Silviano's computer files are poorly organized to say the least, and since we don't know what we're looking for—"

"We'll have to look through everything," I say.

"Yea," she says through gritted teeth of endurance.

"Then let's get to it. Where should I start?"

""Well, I'm going file-by-file through his undescriptively labeled '2013 File.' You could go through his 'Articles and Reviews' cache," she says.

And so the work begins. The 'Article and Reviews' file is Silviano's digital folder of gradually accumulated scholarly articles, books reviews and word document notes written in reaction to the literature he consumes. Silviano takes an argumentative position on nearly every topic, often times his positions contradict themselves from one reaction paper to the next, but he makes no mention of this himself. He invokes science when it is both convenient and useful to justifying his beliefs, but when science poses difficulty or otherwise undermines his personal convictions he's quick to turn to the aid of anecdotal evidence or even the rhetorical trick of equivocation.

"Shit. Shit," Regina says with her eyes glued to her computer screen.

"What? What is it?" I ask.

"Two states, Vermont and New Mexico just passed the AFA," Regina says.

"Damn that's quick," I reply.

"Look, I don't want to get distracted. Let's just stay focused on what we're doing here," Regina says. So we return to our sifting. I know I'll be glad to get through this file. Silviano dogmatically believes that society would be better off without a uniformly agreed upon moral code, that every man should be his own lawmaker. Personally, it seems to me like such a society would more resemble the chaos of the Wild West than it would Thomas More's ethos of Utopia.

"Nothing in the 2013 file. Which file should I search through next?" Regina asks.

"Actually, have you read Silviano's email exchanges with Congressman Callahan?"

"No, no I haven't."

"Well it was Callahan's slip at dinner the other evening that led us to confiscate Silviano's hard drive. See if maybe there isn't a clue in this email," I say.

Regina leans in to her work. A few minutes later she says: "Silviano and Callahan have *a lot* of emails." There's not a hint of exasperation in her voice.

I, on the other hand, am growing tired of concentrating on Silviano's morbid professional interests, with emotionally-charged negatively formulated arguments on every page. This guy has lived his life to criticize and otherwise undermine the work of others. It seems doubtful whether he ever crafted an original, positively formulated argument in his entire life.

"Wylie?"

"Yea?"

"It's after six."

"Oh man it's gotten late. Have we really been working this whole time?"

"We worked right on through lunch."

"Now that you mention it, I'm starving. Wanna get some lunch?"

"You mean dinner? I would, but I really don't think I should. I need to go to school and do a few things to prepare for my class tomorrow. I'll probably just grab something to go along the away."

"I see. Would you at least like for me to walk you?" I can see her feelings on the matter vacillitating.

"Ok, yea. That'd be nice. Just let me pack up here."

Regina gathers her computer and power cord and slides both items in to her sleek leather briefcase, and tosses the strap over her shoulder. I follow her out on to the street. Once we have started walking towards Georgetown's main campus, she readjusts her bag from her right to her left shoulder. I'm also walking on her left. I want to try something, perhaps even a move as innocent as a handhold, but where is my opening? There is a cold and tangible, calculated distance between the two of us. After this thought, I yearn to be closer to her even more. But how close is close enough? Hand holding? Kisses whenever? Snuggling? All-access to the secret's lock-box? Sex? Living together? Marriage? Kids? Can we really ever fully know another person? Hell, I'm scarcely able to predict my own tendencies and behaviors.

"This is me."

"Ok. Don't stay up working too late!"

"Ha," she laughs, fatigue in her voice. "I'm afraid the checking out early option may already be foreclosed."

"Goodnight," I say with a brave smile.

"Thanks Wylie," she says and disappears in to her office building.

I'm working from home today while Regina is teaching her class. I've picked up reading through Silviano and Callahan's email correspondence where Regina left off. Immediately, I'm taken aback by the amount of influence Silviano exercises over Callahan. Callahan asks Silviano to brief him on virtually every hot button political issue. My cell phone buzzes, so I remove it from my pocket to see the message. It's a news update. Five additional states ratified the AFA today. The journalist's commentary goes on to credit the Internet for the proposed constitutional amendment's speedy

178

processing. I take a sip from my coffee cup and feel my heart pounding in my chest and in my head. Anxiety is cutting me on all fronts, like I've crashed through a plate glass window.

The next day, Regina is back to help because she only teaches once a week during the summer. She's beginning to look as stress worn as I am. One additional state convention ratifies the AFA today, with no other states set to hold a vote until at least tomorrow. My phone buzzes. I look down to read the text. It's from Angie:

"It's been a while Wylie, and I haven't heard from you. It looks like I'm going to have a rare evening off, and I was wondering if you might like to meet for dinner and talk?"

Fucking Angie. I've been so absorbed by this case that I haven't even been thinking about her. I glimpse across the coffee table and there's a good reason why. I mean is Regina *really* just casually wearing that dark-tan accentuating tank top and lulemon pants because it's a comfortable outfit? I have no idea where I stand in regards to this girl. Is work icing our burgeoning romance? Or is work our only commonality?

The next morning I wake up to the worst news yet. Ten states are set to vote on and are expected to ratify the AFA. This development will give the AFA half of the assenting states it needs to pass in to law.

"I canceled my class," a text from Regina reads. I hurry over to her apartment to get to work as fast as I can. When I arrive, she's already lost in a rapid-fire trance reviewing file after file. I open my laptop and get to work. We're both laboring away on a prayer that we'll find at least some circumstantial piece of information that will blow this case wide open.

We're both highly disappointed after we've read through *all* of Silviano's and Callahan's email exchanges to uncover not one chard of evidence. At the end of the email chain, we take a break for lo mien and to discuss strategy.

"I guess it makes sense that *if* they did conspire to steal a manuscript they wouldn't just talk about it overtly over their email," Regina says.

"But if there's no smoking gun, no evidence, not even any clues," I say. I'm racking my brain for anything, anything either indicative or suggestive. Did they talk in code? In person? In what other recorded alternative means might they have communicated?

"Did we check the instant messenger history on Silviano's email?" Regina asks.

"No, no I sure didn't. Let's comb through that," I say.

We've only been scanning through these messages for a few moments before I come across the initials AF. "Oh shit, I think I found something."

"What?"

"Look. This message is dated four months ago: 'Sources tell me we may have an AF problem.' That's from Silviano," I say.

"Oh my God," Regina says as she reads on. Chills run down my spine.

Callahan's reply text: "Is it something the wolves can take care of?"

Silviano: "No, it has to be handled much more delicately than that. We need a specialist."

Callahan: "I have one. What's the extent of the clean up?"

Silviano: "We'll need a full job to take care of this mess. To do otherwise is certain to compromise the AFA."

180

Callahan: "Let's meet to discuss."

Silviano: "Ok. Call with a place and time."

The conversation thread breaks off there. I glance over at Regina. A tear is streaming across her face, but she nods confidently. I make a notation of the date of the revealing conversation, then move forward to the approximate time of Al Finkel's death. We both gasp and scoot back when we see the exchange between Silviano and Callahan on the day of Finkel's death. There is no conversation, no words. Hanging there in the history box is a single paper clip, the hyperlink to a single word document attachment. I move the cursor over and click the paper clip. The loading bar appears momentarily exasperated as it uploads a rather large file. Then the screen reads "Download Complete." Then another pop-up screen: "View File or Save for Later?" I click view file and there it is, all 451 pages of it: Al Finkel's last manuscript, The Veracity of Religious History.

"Hit print," Regina says, "*hit print!*"

Chapter 18

Everything begins to happen very quickly following the breakthrough in our investigation. I immediately forward the incriminating message chain between Silviano and Callahan to the lead investigator of Al's homicide. Regina's home printer breaks after she's spun off two full copies of the manuscript, and I save it on every flash drive I can find. I email my principals at Pioneer Publishing to set up a meeting for tomorrow. It's so patently obvious how badly both Regina and I want to read Al's last manuscript, but there's so many real-world issues to be dealt with before I can indulge in the luxury of settling in with a voluminous book. Shortly, Detective Bill Gavern of Washington City Police Department calls me in response to my email.

""Let me talk to Regina," he says. I put the phone on speaker.

"I promise this is real and that I'm not wasting your time," she says. There is a measurable silence and then she says: "I'm more than happy to resolve any of your doubt if you care to drop by and look at the evidence."

"Hmm. I'll tell you what. My partner is out picking up his dry cleaning. Give me your address and we'll roll by after he's returned," the Detective says.

I look over at Regina, who's sitting on the couch thumbing through the manuscript.

"Impatient, are we?" I ask. She drops the manuscript in her lap, covers her face and begins to weep. "No, no it's ok. Read it. You can read it." She shakes her head no. "What is it Regina?" I knell down beside of her and pat her on the leg. After a moment, she begins to dry up.

"They killed him," she says. "They killed him to cover up their deceit and lies. Look, he devoted a whole chapter to describing how they ousted all the honest academics from the AHA, so they could use it as a vehicle to manipulate the population. They violated the most fundamental code of academic ethics."

"Shh," I try to calm her. I move on to the couch to sit beside her. She buries her face in my chest and lets it all out. Soon the police arrive, and Regina dries up long enough to make a statement. When the detectives are done questioning her, she goes to the bathroom to be alone. I finish up, explaining the details and the extent to which the evidence could support a conviction for conspiracy to commit murder. Once the detectives feel they have a satisfactory understanding of the crime, they bundle up all their evidence to return to the station to present the case to their chief and the district's attorney.

The next day I take Al's missing manuscript to the office of Pioneer Publishing. With a three-ring binder filled with manuscript paper tucked under my arm, I am eagerly received by both Lulu and Aaron. They exalt my praises until their wave of excited emotion finally subsides to a sufficient degree to allow them the moment they need to settle down, so we can talk business. They agree to pay me the remainder of the balance on our agreement, plus a $2,500 bonus. They promise to send me as many referrals as they can summon. For me, it's strange how this job evolved from simply hunting down a lost artifact to being sucked in to an ideological vendetta to avenge Al's death and redeem historic neutrality, if not Truth herself.

It takes the criminal justice system a full two days after my and Regina's discovery to begin taking visible action. When it does move; however, it strikes with gail force ferocity. Newsman Bob

Weinghart shows Congressman Callahan's arrest on the House floor on loop on his nightly broadcast, paired with colorful commentary. Callahan's charge: conspiracy to commit murder. Bob also delves into the larger conspiracy, how the villainous AHA collaborated with certain members of Congress to undermine America's traditional Christian—inspired morality and work ethic to destroy the foundations of the American economic order. He goes on to elucidate what tragic social calamity will occur if enough states go on to assent to the ratification of the AFA bill to amend the Constitution. By the week's end, states are both voting against ratification and others are revoking their vote *for* ratification.

Somehow or another, Silviano caught word of his grand jury indictment before they could issue a warrant for his arrest. When the U.S. Marshalls sought him out at his house and office, he was nowhere to be found. My best guess is someone in the criminal justice system tipped him off and he fled the country.

The titans who welded unquestioned control over the AHA resigned from their positions with their reputations permanently marred. All but two were forced to resign from their tenured chairs. Silviano was the only professor officially indicted; none of the other professors could be sufficiently linked to the conspiracy to murder Al Finkel. I spoke with Raul Aquino a few weeks after the news broke; he was pleased to have all of the former members of the AHA readmitted, and to return the body of academics to a democratic-style of governance.

Marred in scandal, proponents of the Affluence for All bill went underground, and conversation over the merits of the law virtually disintegrated overnight. Social discord dissipated, and I can tell walking the streets of D.C. that most of the regular, even-tempered people of D.C. are happy to have this whole controversy behind them.

Chapter 19

After a month of media storm, urgent pleas I take on new cases, assisting prosecutors, and generally trying to hideout and burn one down as often as possible, Regina calls me up one afternoon and asks me to dinner the following evening. I readily accept. During all this time, we have really only seen one another in a professional capacity and always with many others involved. I'm fine with Regina's suggestion we go to Heritage, a local Indian restaurant that's convenient walking distance from my apartment.

I arrive at the establishment earlier than the time of appointment. I feel foolish to be overtly displaying so much excitement, but I just can't help it. I'm silly for this girl, we've recently come through so much, things seemed to be heating up, but now I'm not certain where we stand. I'm fidgeting nervously, standing here near the host's stand, praying the perspiration does not pierce through the cloth of my button-down.

Then I see her ascending the stairs. She's wearing a strappy apricot dress, and it's also apparent she's spared no effort putting her hair up with just a small tuft hanging alluringly across her face. She smiles when she sees me standing here awkwardly, and her freckles set my passion on fire. There's a window of silence now as we stand together alone for the first time in a month.

"Is this your company?" the host asks. "Are you ready to be seated now?"

"Yes," I say. The host gathers two menus and shows us to a table by the window, overlooking the commercial section of Glover Park. Cars gradually stream along Wisconsin Avenue under the large Whole Foods sign. Pedestrians wander the streets just beyond the purview of M Street's throngs of tourists. Glover Park, if removed from the rest of the metropolitan cancer and viewed in isolation, might be a charming, independent township situated somewhere in the vast open spaces of the mid-west.

"It's good to see you Wylie," Regina says.

"Excuse me. I'm sorry, could you say that again?"

"You seem distracted. Is everything ok?"

"I'm sorry. I guess I am distracted. It's the noise of this city. The mania of this way of life. Hhhmm," I exhale. "I apologize for being a downer."

"No, it's fine. Go on."

"It's just, it's just that I've been here for like a decade, pretty much my entire adult life. I guess when I first came here for school I thought this was the place, *the big city*, the capital of the modern world. Res ispa loquitor. But now with all the attention, the very thing every city dweller longs for, I wonder what it would be like to go back home. I wonder what quiet sounds like, without all of the constant hum and hustle, the constant teeth-gnashing."

"You have been thinking a lot."

"Again. I'm sorry to lay this on you. But while I'm speaking frankly, I just want to say that it's really nice to be here with you, alone." Regina moves her hand across the table and places her palm in to my own.

"I've been thinking about you too," Regina whispers. Now a waiter arrives at our table and fills our glasses with water. Perfect timing.

"Welcome to Heritage. Have you eaten with us before?"

"I have," Regina says. I just sit quietly

"We are very glad you have returned. Might I start you with something to drink besides just water?"

"Two Taj Mahals please," Regina says.

"Before I get those drinks for you, would you like to put in an appetizer?"

'Um," Regina hums as she opens and scans the menu. "Um, how about an order of the potato samosas?"

"Excellent choice. I'll give you some time to look over the remainder of the menu and be right back with your beer."

"I'm sorry," Regina says. "I just realized that I didn't even think to ask you if you like Indian food."

"I think I do. I mean, I've lived in DC for ten years," I say and open the menu. "I think I had the tandoori chicken last time, but that's been a while ago."

"Well you got it wrong last time. Let me order for us."

"Order away," I say with a smile, laying my closed menu on the table. "So tell me about school. Doesn't it start back soon?"

"Urgh yes. Next week. I've really fallen behind in planning my class following this whole, I don't know what you call it, I think you used the term 'media storm.' Well, they've virtually got me teaching an entire class this semester. I mean teaching *my own* class. I'm not sure if that's a reward for good deeds or punishment for bringing so much attention to the school. Don't get me wrong, Georgetown loves prestige, the damned place exists for it, but they loath being gossiped about. It's like they only want elites or intellectuals to talk about them, not regular people on the streets."

"It can be a pretty pompous school, but rightfully so. They've earned it over the centuries."

The waiter comes carrying a tray. He places two large beers on the table, glasses, and a basket of what I presume are the potato somosas.

"Now, may I take your orders?"

"Yes, we'll have an order of the makhani butter chicken, the rogan josh lamb, the lemon rice, and an order of garlic nan," Regina says.

"And will that be all?" the waiter asks as he scribbles away on his little pad.

"Yes," Regina says, and we hand him our menus. Then he disappears back towards the kitchen.

"Oh," did I tell you I got offered a book deal?"

"Really?" I ask. "What kind of book?"

"Anything. My pick. This publisher read of couple of academic articles I wrote, saw my name in the news and called me up. Apparently getting published is all about name or brand recognition. It's funny, I'd never really thought of myself as a brand before. Shows how much business sense I have, I suppose."

"Sometimes it's what a person doesn't know that makes her brilliant," I say. Regina blushes before hiding her face behind her napkin.

"Wylie, you've always been so sweet to me."

"You're an easy person to be sweet to; you open yourself up to kindness."

"I'd kiss you if you weren't so far away."

"I can come closer." I say, and Regina nods her head agreeably. I quickly move to a chair closer to Regina at our four-person table. I lean in and peck her on the lips. She rests her hand on my thigh, before leaning in for a more intimate kiss.

"That was nice," she says. After a moment of eye gazing and next move waiting, the waiter and a food runner push a cart up to our table filled with food. The meat-stew type dishes are in a bowl atop an extension that harbors lit candles. Regina shows me how she eats it, first padding her plate with a helping of rice before drizzling

189

the stew over top like gravy. Once I start eating, I realize what an appetite I've got and how damned good this Indian food is. It's an easy reminder of one of the great positive aspects of DC: it's the world brought to me in one place. Now I know there are Indian restaurants all across the country, but my point is that few places have the scale of diversity as DC.

After dinner, I pay the bill, and Regina and I begin walking in the general direction towards her place without any meaningful discussion of where it is we're going. We're in this rare type of giddy mood that makes everything around you seem silly, laughable, and absolutely amazing. It's a moment when it's easy to appreciate the simple pleasures. A moment when you feel the warmth of existence, creation, and God. It's like understanding on a higher plane than everyday ordinary awareness. The frequency of our kissing increases the closer and closer we get to Regina's apartment. By the time we reach her door, we're full on making out. She drops her keys twice while trying to unlock the door. Finally, we bust in to her unlit living room. She pushes me over the arm of her couch, and I fall on my back, landing safely on the cushions. I hear the door shut and the dead bolt lock. I sit up to see where she's gone, but suddenly I find her lying on top of me. Through my nose is the only way I can gather breath. I have a little laugh to myself, at all the tribulations of the last month, at the truly rough, depressing moments. I didn't understand the purpose of the hardship then, nor did my consciousness pierce the veil of the suffering, but in this moment I appreciate it all. The struggle is merely the contrast that makes moments like this so sweet.

Mountainlion Press would like to thank you for reading our novel. Please provide your comments, praise or critique for this book on either its amazon.com salespage or on Goodreads. Your feedback helps us produce literature of higher quality and in greater abundance.